THE BOY TOYS OF PARIS

A NOVEL

ERIC REESE

CONTENTS

ISBN: 9781925988314

Human trafficking comes in all forms. My job is to bring forth its hidden identity in words.

"I don't design clothes. I design dreams."

RALPH LAUREN

ENCHANTÉ

OVERJOYED!

Today was our team's football match. I was breathing heavy stressed that we were on a three-game losing streak. Would we lose again? It's possible. My teammates weren't playing good, and I was barely training these days; hurt by a knee collision with another player a few weeks back. For the most part, we played well together until our top player, Sudi went down due to injury. I made a promise to myself to play harder this week.

This match meant a lot to me. If we lost, I'd let my father down. I gripped the handle of my duffel bag and hurried into the dressing room, already seeing my teammates joking around.

"It's about time you made it, Abbasi. Coach wants to see you." Demond rolled his eyes as he passed by, walking out of the locker room in a hurry. He never liked me, and the feeling of hatred was mutual. The rest of the team didn't bother looking my way as they got dressed. I took off my jacket, wasting no time in getting dressed in our team's kit.

I had second thoughts whether Demond was telling the truth, but still I had to go by Coach's office. I knocked twice on the door and waited. He was sitting at his desk, buried in the newspaper.

Strangely, he read it every day three times. The man was obsessed someday his team might be featured somewhere inside. I guess that was what motivated him. From the corner of his eye, he saw me come and put it down.

"You wanted to see me, Coach?" I stated, awkwardly standing outside the door.

"Yeah, come on in." He cleared his throat, waiting for me to close the door. "Are you prepared for today?"

My silence irked him and he let out a loud groan of desperation, balling his fists as if he wanted to punch me. I wasn't the best player on the team, nor was I the worst. He could depend on me on most occasions. I think the potential he saw in me was the only thing that he cared about.

"You know I'm not fit these days, Coach. It's hard balancing my family duties and the team's." I said avoiding his stare while looking down at my old cleats. I couldn't afford to buy a new pair.

"Is that my fault? You know damn well Sudi can't play. I need you to step up." Sudi broke his ankle and was the best player on the team. If you would have saw this old man's eyes when he said that, you would have thought Sudi was the Cullinan diamond.

"Tell me the truth. Do you no longer want to play?" Coach took a packet of cigarettes from his drawer, lighting one while focusing was on me.

"I do. You know I do, but as you can see, Coach, my body just doesn't seem to be healthy these days. I need rest."

"So, you will give in just like that?" He said not believing a word I said.

I was telling the truth. I wasn't going to waste my time on something which might never work out and may leave me injured for life.

———

The capital city where I'm from is named Douala. It's not too populated, and we don't have the football star power like other African countries. There are a few boys who got recognized by scouts who made it to Europe. Even our national team are truly embraced even though we won the African Cup of Nations five times. I was a no-name footballer, as pathetic as it might sound. Eventually, I'll come to grips with myself that helping my family is first and foremost, but what road would I choose to do it remains a mystery? All I see ahead of me at the moment was a never-ending loop of misery and it was getting worse by the day.

"I have amateur talent. The only thing I do well is let my parents down," I said to Coach.

Coach stood up, ready to hit me with the newspaper.

"You will not give up that easily. Over my dead body, young man."

I moved back quickly and raised my hands in defence. If I had to, I would fight back. Coach had some old heavy hands and his punches probably would put me in the hospital for weeks.

"All right, Coach. I was just joking." I grinned, trying to ease the situation. He was ready to fight, but as soon as I saw him shake his head, I knew he was okay.

"I don't want to hear those words from you again, Abbasi. You have the looks. The skill will come. Look at all these famous African football players. Most of them made it because of their looks, not because of talent. Be confident in yourself. The match starts in thirty minutes. Get going."

"Yes, Coach."

I sprinted back to the lockers. None of my teammates were there, so they were out on the field warming up.

I grabbed my water bottle, dressed and ran out to the field. There wasn't an open spot in the training circle. I felt so bad that I wasn't prepared and no on time.

Was I going to be able to give it my all today? While deep in concentration, I didn't notice Elon come right next to me.

"You ready?" He said with a comforting smile.

I nodded back hoping that God would be with me throughout the whole match. Coach would be pissed if I didn't play well.

"I had a lot to do lately, so I haven't been training

much." I mentioned as we walked towards the bench where the other teammates were seated.

"Just try your best," he advised, giving me a nudge on the shoulder.

"Of course." I said as both teams were waiting for the referee to blow his whistle.

Once our opponents gathered, my nerves rose. I feared that I would mess up. Coach came to the bench, signalling for us to get up. He assembled us in a circle, double-checking our positions. I listened closely but my mind was somewhere else. My teammates were eager to play and kept nodding their heads at him.

Before I knew it, we were running on the field and lining up. The whistle from the referee signalled. *It's time to start.* The ball ended up on their side, and it felt like the odds were already stacked against us.

I ran to the side, taking position on defense. The player I was guarding was fast but I remained focused. I was defending him perfectly. He did a drag back with the ball and I was unable to come up with it. I was pissed for letting that chance slip through my fingers.

"Abbasi, what are you doing?" Elon yelled, angrily.

I waved him off and didn't notice I lost my player. *Where is he?* I panicked trying to get back to him and missed the opportunity from stopping him from scoring a goal. What a mess! They didn't deserve that one.

The crowd cheered and celebrated. I got frustrated looks from my teammates and Coach. The game continued. I was determined to block out everything. Focusing on my opponent, I was able to steal the ball this time, quickly volleying it to my teammate.

We were inching closer towards our opponents' goal. Demond was in the front attack and passed the ball back to me which I relayed it quickly to Camar. Demond signalled Camar to pass the ball back, outrunning the player who was guarding him. Once Demond got a hold of the ball, he outran his defender towards the goal and scored.

The team jumped in joy and crowd joined the celebration including Coach who looked over at me and pumped up his fist in air.

My anxiety grew when it was time to start again. Would I be able to assist another goal? I didn't want to let Coach down. When my man headed towards the goal, roughly dribbling the ball. I quickened my pace and ran side to side. With every move he did, I wasn't able to get the ball. The attention was on us and both teams were betting their hopes on one of us to succeed. I did everything possible to stop him including pushing him too hard; he landed on the ground, yelling in pain.

I was given my first red card ever and Coach was ready to kill me. Furiously, he subbed out another player to change strategies now we were down to ten men.

Once the half-time whistle blew, everyone on my team directed their insults towards me. I would be lying if I said I didn't feel offended. I probably would have done the same.

"Abbasi, what's the hell is wrong with you?" Coach screamed, not holding himself back.

"I'm sorry, Coach." I didn't know what to say.

"You will be on the bench for three games. Lord have mercy son. You have killed us!"

I felt bad. Yaro came in at half-time replacing another player. He was a weaker player. Although in the past months, he'd been trying to prove himself. Maybe this is the match where Coach would consider him playing for time. The score was tied 1-1.

Coach lectured the team using my mistake as a way to push the team to win the game. I had doubts, but sat eager to see the outcome. The minute the referee whistled for the start of the second half, Coach sat next to me, yet strangely didn't say a word. Should I say something? Nope. I'd piss him off for sure. We sat in silence and watched the game closely until our opponents scored another goal and again he cursed aloud, kicking the dirt all around. 2-1.

He was in rage, looking at me as if I brought hell to our pitch.

"Don't bother coming back to the team if you don't train properly."

"Yes, sir." I didn't talk back. I knew I lost the game for us.

My team's faces were worn out. They couldn't believe that this weak team defeated them. I was almost expected defeat since I didn't train well. At the ending whistle, we shook hands with the other team's players and huddled vowing we would win the next match.

Honestly, my father never wanted me to play football. In his eyes, I didn't have enough talent and could injure myself severely. He wanted me to find something I could be good at. Somehow, I believed that football was what I was good at and if I kept pushing myself, I could be a good player. For now, it looked like I gave up.

"What's happening to you all out there? You're getting killed on the pitch." Coach said with a bit of sympathy. He did so every time we lost. We've gotten used to being losers since Sudi broke his ankle. It was for the best to keep quiet during Coach's rants. But there was still that 'better luck next time' feeling that Coach hated for us to say. All the players said it behind his back but they weren't concerned with winning. In the end, I think Coach was losing faith in us.

As the bleachers cleared, so did everyone on the pitch. I was the only one who remained behind, thinking hard about my next steps. How would I tell this to my father? He had such high hopes for me. I began pulling my beard, trying to release my anger.

"May I join you?" a female voice softly spoke, cutting me out of my agony. I looked up and saw a blonde woman standing over me. Her blonde hair was plunged over her shoulders and her slender eyebrows were raised waiting for my answer. She was a white woman, an outsider.

"Oh, yeah, sure." I awkwardly answered, still staring

at her puzzled. Her dainty nose was the only thing I noticed from her face until I looked at her expensive clothes. Was she a tourist here? What could she possibly be looking for in a old football field like this?

"I saw you playing out there. You seem to be struggling a bit."

What does this woman want? "I'm not fit to play right now." This woman was a lot older than I, almost close to the age of my mother's younger sister.

"I can see that. Why? Do you not have any motivation?"

I frowned, staring at her. "I like football, ma'am but sometimes it feels like I put too much effort into it and wind up getting injured all so frequently." What's the name of this stranger? I kept thinking.

She then crossed her legs and then pulled a cigarette out, lighting it up and exhaling. The horrific smell bothered me.

"What's your dream then?" she asked. Why did she ask this? I chuckled not giving her an answer right away. Honestly, I didn't even know the answer myself.

"I'll figure it out along the way I guess, but for now I want to have a good paying job." I said standing, ready to leave.

Before so, she grabbed my arm causing me to stop moving. "What if I had a good paying job to offer you?" I looked down at her, seeing a crooked smile on her face. Like what I thought?

"I'm sorry ma'am but I don't know you and I'm not

interested in selling drugs or being a boy toy," I said pulling myself away, but her grasp got stronger.

"Oh boy, please. I'm not here to offer you illegal things. By the way, I'm Anna and it's nice to meet you." She wanted to shake my hand but I hesitated. In our culture, we don't shake womens' hands.

I gave it some thought but then fell compelled to do so.

"I'm Abbasi. It's nice to meet you." I smiled weakly. This woman was attractive, and I wasn't so sure if I could trust her.

"You mentioned you needed a well-paying job. I'm going to make you an offer and it's up to you whether you agree or not." She sighed.

I nodded. "Okay." I was ready to listen.

"I'm a contractor for a modelling agency in France. They send me all over the world to recruit new top models. If you say yes, you could be one."

Her statement took me by surprise. "Me, a model?" I've never seen myself as someone being in front of the cameras and magazines, let alone walking runways. I didn't have an attractive face, nor the body of a someone who was extremely fit.

"I'm not good for that job, sorry to break it to you." It has taken me many years to learn how to play football. I couldn't even guess how many more I would need to become a model.

"You'll learn and we'll train you. It's only a science of

posture and beauty. You have the looks to do the job, sweetheart."

Could I trust her? There was a lot of swindling in my city even involving the foreigners.

"I don't know if…"

She cut me off. "Don't give me an answer right away. This job can pay up to three thousand euros per month. Here is my business card. Call the number on it as you make up your mind. I'll be expecting your call." She gave me a final smile as she handed me it to me. It read *'New Era Modelling Agency'* in bold golden letters. Her name, phone number and email were written neatly on it. I put it in my back pocket, not giving it much value.

Back in the locker room, everyone had already dressed and left. I took a few minutes to reflect on the offer from the blonde woman.

Should have I decided right away? I was afraid of making a wrong choice. The fear of my parents dawned on me. Dad wanted me to quit football and join him at his job, but I declined many times.

I packed up my things and came home; seeing my parents and sister watching television in the front of the compound with some neighbours. I didn't want to tell them about the offer or my team losing today.

"Hey Abbasi, how was the match?" My sister Imani asked. I lowered my head, and they all knew what that meant; we lost again.

"I knew it. I don't know why you're wasting your time

playing for that stupid team. Football isn't for you." Dad looked frustrated.

It wasn't the time to argue with him. He worked long shifts putting food on the table and paying our bills. I disappointed him by losing matches. Ignoring him wasn't the best thing either.

"I didn't train, Dad. I've been dealing with a knee injury a few weeks back. For the next match, I'm sure we will win." I left them outside while I went to the kitchen, pouring myself a glass of water.

"You won't win because there won't be a next time. It's finished. You're done playing football." As soon as those words left his mouth, I was shocked. Football was my only hope of getting out of this country. How could he?

"You can't do this to me", I yelled back in anger.

"I can because it's about time you come to your senses." His face turned redder than Mars.

"Dad, listen. I put effort into it. You need to believe in me. I will be one of the best." I tried convincing him but all I got was the cold shoulder. I couldn't work with him delivering goods across the city in a hot van all day.

"By the way, I received an offer to start modelling in France this afternoon."

Everyone suddenly became silent. "Maybe I shouldn't have said that?" Even a minute later, no one said a word.

When I was heading to my room, that's when my

sister came to me and said "Are you serious? Who offered you this job?"

"What are you two talking about back there?" Dad interrupted, coming while Mom was right behind him.

They didn't know how to react to the news.

"Yeah, it's true. I got a job today and I probably will agree to it." I said while clutching the woman's card in my back pocket. I needed to show them that I could be a responsible young adult for once.

"Abbasi, stop messing around, you're not going to leave this country until you have a decent education?" Dad shook his head, now taking a seat at the table. "Find a decent job, get married, and have children. Your mother and I aren't asking for much." His eyes pleading as if someone had tired him out named Abbasi.

"It's a well-paying job. Why wouldn't I agree to do it?" I replied, sitting down.

"How do you know if the agents are trustworthy? Have you seen what's going on in the news here? So many of these young men and women are being scammed by these so-called recruiters. Some have even come as far as Iran offering land and wealth to promote their ideology here." Dad had a point, yet there was something about this job that made me believe that it was credible.

"Who offered you the job?" Imani repeated.

I looked at Dad and Mom expecting my answer. "A white woman named Anna came to our match and approached me afterwards."

Everyone looked confused. I was a twenty-year old kid for God's sake and my parents didn't believe they can fully trust me yet.

"Did she say anything else?" Mom asked.

"She gave me a business card, Mom. Look." I reached in my pocket and showed it to her. Everyone looked at it closely. Dad didn't know much about emails, so I was sure he'd have second thoughts and Mom didn't trust no one outside of Cameroon. Not even the Nigerians.

"They will pay three thousand euros a month. A lot of money." The money wouldn't be a lot in France, but in Cameroon, it'll be a fortune.

"I don't know Abbasi. This sounds fishy. I don't want you to get yourself in trouble. However, we support you no matter what you chose. The only thing we ask is that you chose wisely, son." Mom said smiling cautiously. Dad didn't add anything else.

———

Later that evening, I planned on giving Anna a call. I paced around my room, scared to press the call button. Somehow, I kept becoming distracted and kept delaying. "What if someone else takes the offer?" I couldn't stop hesitating.

I sighed in frustration and needed to make the call once and for all. Once I pressed the call button, there was no turning back. After three rings, a soft woman's voice answered. "Hello?"

"Hello Madame. This is Abbasi. You gave me your card this afternoon after my match about the modelling job. Do you remember?"

There was a pause then she replied. "Abbasi, oh dear. What have you decided?"

I shut my eyes tightly ready to announce that I will work accept the offer. This would change my life forever, and I would make my parents proud.

"I agree to your job offer. I'm ready to start working."

"I'm very happy to hear that, Abbasi. I will email the necessary information about the job and documentation required to travel to France."

"Wow! What would my parents and sister say now that I've accepted the job?" My mere thoughts as she talked.

"Can you tell me when you would need me to travel? I need to prepare." I said while hearing some shuffling by Anna over the line.

"Well, we will probably need you to come to France a week from now. You and another Cameroonian will leave on the same date. You'll meet each other at the airport. That's all the information I can give you for now. I'll email you with everything in the next following days. Take care, Abbasi." With that, she hung up. I texted her my email address shortly after and laid down on my bed.

A model from Cameroon? My countrymen would joke at the idea. Modelling was regarded for only women here. I peeked outside my door to see if anyone was still awake. It seems as if my news had caused them to fall asleep.

Working in France next week? It was hard for me for me to sleep at the mere thought. Where would this adventure take me?

The next morning came quickly. I woke up too early. The first thing I did was check my email. I was anxious to tell my parents I agreed to the contract.

I entered the kitchen smiling, seeing everyone sitting at the table. They stopped talking as soon as they saw me enter.

"I'm going to be a model."

Imani clasped her hands together in excitement. Mom jumped up in joy and was the first to hug me. Dad shook his head and continued reading the newspaper.

"Aren't you going to congratulate me, Dad?" I pressed, feeling entitled.

He flashed a smile but then it faded as he turned away. "If you call that a real job, I congratulate you."

He was being sarcastic but I was happy with his blessing. I sat down eating in union. I couldn't wait to tell my friends and Coach. I'm sure they'd be happy for me and a little bummed at the same time. Who knows, maybe I could take them to France someday or help them out.

"Mom, I'm going out to visit some of my friends and tell them the good news."

"Come home early tonight, son. I'll prepare your

favourite meal" Mom said. She was filled with joy and did this on special occasions. Today must be one. A well-paying job in France could solve a whole lot of our problems.

———

The week quickly passed, and I was treated like a king. Anna sent me an email three days ago explaining what I needed and that my paperwork had already be expedited. She paid for my passport, visa and told me to work out for a few days with her before arriving to Paris. I also found out that my flight to Paris was already paid for as well. This would be an experience worth documenting.

"I have everything. You need not worry." I told Mom worried that I wasn't prepared.

"Abbasi, do you know where you even will stay? I need to make sure you will be okay." Mom said as she closed my suitcase. Mom is always right.

"You're all set and good to go. Go on now my boy and may God be with you. Dad's waiting in the car." She picked up my luggage, putting it on top of her head. The old woman refused my help, saying it was the least she could do to help. Dad would take me to the airport since he had deliveries nearby afterwards.

I said my goodbyes to Mom and Imani, kissing them both on the foreheads. Both were sobbing at the sight of me leaving.

"Hurry up, Abbasi. You'll be late." Dad yelled from

the car. I gave them one last hug and ran outside; throwing my stuff in the back.

———

The traffic was light as we headed down the main highway to Douala International Airport. Anna texted me with a picture of the guy who I'd meet. He would be holding up a sign with my name on it. I was sure I'd recognise him right away.

Days earlier, she outlined my expenses. The only thing I needed to buy was street clothes and personals. Since the company paid for food, gym memberships, accommodation and utilities, I didn't have to spend much.

"Do you know where you'll be staying?" Dad asked as we speeding up.

"In a nice condominium. Two guys will be staying there with me. One from Italy and another from here."

He nodded in approval but I could sense his uneasiness. He feared I'd would get scammed or worse. How could I convince him otherwise? Dad always had to be right.

Dad arrived to the departure gate. He parked to the curb and pressed the button to open the back door.

"Take care, son. If something doesn't seem right, come home."

I gave him a tight hug and then exited, taking my suitcases from the back and closing the doors. He watched me until I got inside. I couldn't look back, so I waved from behind. I was determine to make my family proud.

As I entered, I noticed the airport was jam packed. I didn't know what gate my plane departed from, so I went to customer service and stood in line.

I handed the servicewoman my tickets. "My flight is leaving in about an hour and a half. I'm going to Paris; do you know what gate I'm supposed to go to?" The lady smiled and searched on her computer.

She directed me towards a check-in in the rear near the second floor elevator. I thanked her and left, thinking about the whereabouts of the other guy. Hopefully, I'd recognise him or else I would leave without him.

Sitting down, I watched people passing by, hoping to identify the guy by the name of *Jafari*.

After fifteen minutes of looking for someone with a sign who didn't show up, I got nervous. "Maybe I'll have a peep at New Era's website. What else is there to do?" On the site, there were models posing for different occasions. There were also videos of them walking on runways and taking pictures with global celebrities. Maybe that will be me in a few months. I laughed at the mere thought.

Just when I got tired of looking, a person sat down next to me and said in a soft tone, "Are you, Mr. Abbasi?" I looked up seeing the same man in the picture that Anna emailed.

I jumped to my feet extending my hand. "Yes, it's nice to meet you."

"Nice to meet you likewise. I'm Jafari." He said shaking my hand. We sat down and waited for our flight to be called.

I tried to make small talk, but he didn't seem interested until I asked, "By way, Jafari. How did Anna discover you?"

"I was playing tennis with a friend. She came one afternoon to a match and told me about the position." Jafari sounded so proud of himself.

"How about you Have you modelled before?"

I shook my head in disbelief, laughing. "No, my friend. She approached me at a match as well."

"I see. She must have a thing for sports. I mean it doesn't surprise me. She was so observant about my match. I thought she might have been a professional tennis player at one time."

That was a nice, but Anna did the exact same thing after my match. What a coincidence!

"Ladies and gentleman, Flight 119 is now boarding." The announcement echoed throughout the airport. That was our flight.

"We should get going." Jafari had his bags in his hands, ready to board.

"Yeah, let's go." We proceeded to stand in line waiting for the attendant to take our tickets and checked our luggage. After a few minutes, all of the passengers boarded. Jafari and I discovered that our seats were in first-class. *Wow!*

Jafari talked as if he flew many times before but this was his first time. I started feeling nauseous. Peeking out of the window, I couldn't believe the beauty of the clouds how they covered us. We would be in Paris in about eight and a half hours. Within minutes, the plane reached altitude.

I took a long deep breath. It was a goodbye to Douala, and a welcoming hello to Paris.

———

Paris's scenery was magical. The minute Jafari and I left the airport, the welcoming atmosphere of the Parisians impressed us. We didn't feel like strangers. The taxi driver spoke in a French dialect we didn't recognise, leaving us struggling to understand one another.

"Bonjour! "You gentlemen will have a lovely time here. I promise. You'll stay a long time. A short vacation is not enough time for this beautiful Villé."

"We'll be in town for awhile. Do you have any recommendations on where we should visit?" Jafari asked.

I nodded, eager to hear what the driver would say.

"You already know the Eiffel Tower, but if you have time you need to visit the Paris Catacombs. To this day whenever I go there, I get the chills." Jafari and I looked at each other; signalling our approval.

As we continued to drive around, I saw the grand

facades of the French buildings. I've always seen them on TV, but now I could say I saw them in person. Jafari and I took pictures, never getting enough of the sights.

We split the cost of the ride and the driver was nice enough to unloaded our suitcases on the other side of the street building. I forgot to say goodbye and tip him. The beauty of the apartment building dazed me.

"You coming or not?" Jafari called me from the other side of the street. "Yeah." I cleared my throat, grabbed my belongings and walked. He rang the intercom, waiting in suspense.

A female voice answered, "New Era Modelling Agency. How may I help you?"

"Hello. My colleague and I just arrived from Cameroon for the modelling job. Your agent Anna sent us here and we just arrived from the airport."

"Your names, please?" You can tell she was chewing bubble gum and wasn't paying attention.

"Jafari Ironsi and…" He paused looking at me.

"Abbasi Ademola," I finished his sentence.

"Just a minute." She turned off the intercom while we waited for the next minute until the front gate buzzed.

Once inside, we passed by a huge courtyard filled with many types of plants. There was a security guard standing, who welcomed us.

"Walk straight ahead" We continued straight until we reach a second entrance. Its sliding doors opened revealing a reception desk, with an attractive blonde standing behind it, with a big smile on her face.

"Welcome. How may I help you?"

"Yes, my partner and I are here for the modelling job."

She nodded, dialling a number.

"This way." She announced as she declined a phone call and then led us to the elevator which took us to another floor. We arrived to a room which was nicely decorated. The walls were white, and the chandeliers in it were crystalising. I wondered how much did they cost for some reason.

"Will we be staying here?" I asked.

The lady didn't directly answer my question.

"On the last floor, you will meet lots of new guys like yourselves. You're many this time around." She smiled and opened a door on her left, leading us to a bigger office with decorations on the wall.

There was no one inside. She stood and told us to remain silent. Our eyes inspected the room as we waited in suspense.

There was a mahogany desk in the middle of the room. The windows were clear revealing downtown buildings with heavy traffic. The sunlight from its top pierced into the ceiling of the room. Surrounding the desk, were couches made of leather. Never in my life have I ever seen an office like this.

An another woman then appeared and then left. "Pauline will be here in a minute. Make yourselves comfortable."

"How many models do you think are new like us?"

Jafari asked.

"I don't know." said the receptionist who escorted us. She thanked us for coming and then left as well.

"Maybe twenty tops." Jafari said leaning back, making himself comfortable.

I shook my head, laughing. "How many rooms do you think are in this building?"

"Hmm. Probably more than fifty."

Suddenly, we heard a woman clearing her throat from a door in the rear. We looked over to see who might it be. "She must be the boss." I thought.

"My name is Pauline. I'm the CEO of New Era Modelling Agency. Nice to meet you gentlemen."

"Thank you, Madame." We replied.

"We've been expecting you. May I offer you anything to drink?"

We declined and offered our thanks.

"So, gentlemen. How was your flight?" She asked while looking at some documents in her hands. I looked at Jafari to speak first.

"It was our first time on an airplane, Madame. It was weird at first but we enjoyed the flight." He said stuttering as she giggled.

"It's good to hear that you made it in one piece. Now onto business. Are you prepared for your modelling careers?"

Would she would send me back home if she saw I wasn't ready? I looked her straight in the eye hoping she would see that I'm serious.

"Huh, we don't quite know what the job requires but we're willing to learn. Anna mentioned a training session, but we were given the plane tickets right away to come. Hopefully you will turn us into promising models." I said stuttering throughout.

"No worries, my dears. My secretary will fill you in on the trainings in the morning. I'm sure you're very tired, am I right?"

We nodded hoping we gave her a good first impression.

"Trisha come to my office, now." She told someone on the phone.

The young woman who came in earlier returned. Her appearance suited to the image of the agency. Pauline was far more stylish being she was the CEO.

"Jafari and Abbasi, come with me please." We stood up, thanking Pauline, who gave us a smile back. Then we were taken to an elevator, up to the fourth floor. Trisha chatted with us the whole time before reaching our quarters.

"There is a single bathroom inside. We know it could be a bit uncomfortable sharing. All the other accommodations are full at the moment. Here are your keys."

We were at Room 25.

"There's a guy here who came two months ago. I'm sure you'll get along just fine with Mr. Zane," she said as she unlocked the door, revealing a decorated room with three beds spaced out.

"Wow," Jafari exhaled.

The walls were painted dark red, and the wooden floors were shiny. The windows were transparent gleaming from the sunlight.

Trish took off before we could turn around and thank her. "This is amazing, better than I expected." Jafari said smiling, plopping himself down on one of the empty beds.

"Why are you so quiet, Abbasi? Aren't you impressed?" He said while unpacking his stuff.

I shrugged, feeling grateful. "It's nice I guess." I responded.

Where's our roommate? I guess we will meet him soon enough. We had the rest of the evening to ourselves, so I planned on arranging my area and getting some rest.

Jafari played some games on his tablet while I went out on the balcony to get a view of the scenery.

Was I lucky? It felt like I hit the jackpot. God continues to bless me in such mysterious ways.

"Damn, the city looks amazing." I shouted as Jafari came and joined me.

It was more beautiful than anything I ever saw before. I wondered what my family were doing, hoping they were okay. Hopefully, they're taking my absence well. I'll send them some money soon.

———

The next morning, I was awakened up by a loud knock. I didn't sleep well due to sleeping in a different bed.

Slowly, I dragged towards the door and opened it. There was a European guy standing at the door, carrying a duffel bag. He looked at me, putting his phone in his pocket.

"You must be my new roommate." He smiled, letting himself in and passing by. "Roommates," he corrected himself after he saw Jafari stretched out on the bed.

I felt awkward. "Yeah, we arrived yesterday afternoon. I'm Abbasi."

"Zane."

"That's Jafari,"

Zane didn't seem interested in talking further. I suppose he'd been out partying, judging from his tired appearance.

So, this is what it was like, I thought. I would be restless while spending time here.

Jafari woke up thirty minutes later, introducing himself to Zane. Zane invited us to go down together for breakfast. The cafeteria started serving around 8 a.m. The layout of the cafeteria reminded me of my old high school days.

"Zane, come over here, big man!" Someone shouted from a group at the furthest end of the cafeteria. He joined them, leaving us.

"Where do we sit?" I said while standing in line waiting for our food. We looked around to find an empty table but all were taken.

I ordered a burger and fries. I turned around and saw

all of boys eating salads and protein shakes. So embarrassing! For today, I will dig in.

We spotted an empty table and Zane waved his hand for us to come over. Looking like total rejects, we were compelled to go over to him.

Jafari hurried, eager to sit down and eat. I took my time, thinking how I should introduce myself. I had to make a strong first impression.

"These are the new recruits who came yesterday." Zane said as he ate.

"The name's Abbasi," I blurted, sitting down.

"Where are you from?" one guy asked.

"Cameroon." I responded with pride, thinking that they didn't know where that was.

"Nice," another guy said.

"We're from London mate." The group answered.

"I'm Daniel and the rest of the fuckers, you don't need to know who they are."

Everyone laughed.

Each guy said his name and we nodded.

Daniel seemed friendly. I'm not sure if I have time to make friends. I can already sense these boys and their back-biting ways. Everyone wants to outshine one another. Modelling was all about prestige. But what was prestige in this case? Everyone here are considered amateurs.

"Except for me. I'm from Verona, Italy." Zane made sure he was last in the conversation. I heard a little about the city he's from a local Cameroonian footballer. I think

Zane knew more about modelling than us being that he's from Italy.

Jafari had a lot of questions about London. I didn't pay much attention, just sitting there listening. I wondered how long they've been working for New Era. Nothing came up about that during their conversations.

"So enough about us, tell us about Cameroon." Daniel said, eager to know.

"It's just a small country, nothing too fancy," I replied. They would belittle us if they knew we came from the ghetto.

Jafari gave me a look, but I ignored. I focused on eating and wasn't interested in small talk at the moment. Was it the best decision? I wasn't sure, but I respected Jafari for caring and continuing the conversation after I spoke.

As we were finishing up, Trisha came to the cafeteria, clapping her hands to get our attention. "The new guys, down the main hall in ten minutes. The rest back at the studio." With that, she left walking down the hall. Behold, we got our first job.

I pulled Jafari, being the first ones to leave the cafeteria. "There is some sort of competition going around here, can't you see it?"

"What are you talking about, bro?"

"Well, I guess you can't see it. You're making quick friends with the Brits. They think they're better than everybody. Look how they carry themselves." We tried to find the main hall, looking around everywhere.

Jafari chuckled. "Are you serious, man? Better than everybody else?" He said, almost tripping.

"If I came from London I would too, plus they've been here longer than us."

I rolled my eyes. Finally, we found it after walking in circles. Once we arrived, we were the first ones to arrive.

"Just keep your distance. I wouldn't trust them."

"There is no fitting in here. We're all on the same team, so just chill out." I didn't know if he was being naïve or straight up stupid. Maybe both.

The main hall became swarmed with more newbies who resembled boys at a new school; all were looking around puzzled. There was a great sense of excitement. Once everyone was present, we were told to be seated. The doors were closed by a tall woman and man wearing fancy outfits. They gracefully walked towards the runway while the other staff members made room for them to pass by, not looking at any of us.

"Welcome to New Era, prospective models. This'll be your first training session. I am Francois and this is Ines. We will be your mentors." The crowd cheered and clapped. Jafari joined them, while I remained focused, listening in.

"As you may already know you've been recruited from many countries around the world with the vision of becoming the next supermodels of France." His words caused an uproar. "All of us here, supermodels? Please don't make me laugh." I thought aloud.

"Now, your first job is to walk down this runway.

Many of you may think it's easy, but it isn't. The runway is the only way to show how you will do in front of the world." Next, the woman spoke, resembling a model herself.

"Francois is going to show you how not to walk down a runway." She motioned for Francois to demonstrate. He faked a horrible walk which caused everyone to laugh. I even chuckled. "Who in their right mind would walk like that?"

Jafari looked nervous. "What's wrong with you?"

"Nothing. I've never done this before and don't know if I can." He said scratching his head.

"It's only walking. Just do it with confidence. It can't be that hard. Probably something we can learn in minutes." I said confidently.

"We have a list of your names, and we'll call you up here one by one to see you walk." Francois announced.

"Okay, first up is Diego Montolla." There was a sudden silence as all of us were glad we weren't the first. A man stood up and walked towards the stage, trembling. He couldn't look anyone in the eye.

"You are free to walk. DJ, please turn up the music."

Diego looked scared to death. The music came on. He wasn't pacing well as he stumbled a few times, almost falling on his face. I covered my mouth trying not to laugh, hoping Diego would get it together.

He continued walking with baby steps, looking around. That was worse. Some of the boys laughed, showing him no support and the look on Ines's face was devastating. It looked like there wasn't any hope for him.

"You can stop now, Diego. Thank you." She didn't bother looking at him and cleared her throat, calling up the next person on the list. Diego was crushed. What an embarrassment! Nobody tried to console him out of fear that he would be associated with him.

"Will Alan, come up." Francois called looking around the crowd.

"Me!" One guy in the crowd yelled, excitedly that it was his turn. He ran up to the stage in excitement. He seemed ready for the moment.

The music started, and he started his strut down the runway. The only flaw I saw was his missing teeth. He kept smiling too much.

"He's bad, isn't he?" Jafari mumbled.

I shrugged. "Could have been worse. He needs to wipe that damn smile off his face."

Ines didn't seem to like his performance, but she applauded.

"We can do this." I gave Jafari some words of encouragement. This was a piece of cake. How complicated can this be?

Will went back to his seats, receiving multiple handshakes from others. Then a few more went up. Most of those guys were making too many mistakes and weren't model material. Only one or two actually did well. I didn't know anything about modelling, but I knew enough to say that these guys look like shit.

"Abbasi Ademola," Ines announced. My name echoed the hall's wall, raising attention. The lady actually pronounced my name correctly.

Jafari patted me on the back. "Good luck." I strutted towards the runway confident I'd do okay. All eyes were on me. I couldn't mess up.

"Once you're ready." Francois spoke. I was ready, but the bright crystal ball above us was blinding my sight. No wonder why no one could focus with that thing burning on their faces. Would it always be like that? The music started playing and I began.

I looked serious, but I added a slight smile in the middle of my walk to spice things up. Francois and Ines stared at me and I couldn't judge their reactions to my performance. They didn't show any emotion.

When I finished, they clapped for me as well as the others. I stepped off the runway feeling great and couldn't help but smile. Once I got back to my seat, Jafari grabbed my face laughing. "You were amazing, man. You have some talent."

"Just walk naturally. Don't overdo it," I advised.

"When I first got up there, I feared everything but realised it's only a competition. Fear is for losers."

I had to be the favourite, no matter what.

They called Jafari next. He was tense, afraid to look up and meet Francois and Ines's eyes. Once he began, he wasn't all that bad. Just needed not to look ahead and not move his head so much. I thought they liked him and seemed pleased with his performance.

There was no feedback, only notes written down in Francois and Ines's notebooks.

"All right, we're will be completely honest with you. We expected more, but thank God, there's time for improvement." Ines said glancing at her notes. Francois commented as well saying the same. They were our mentors, so we trusted their judgement.

"You will practice every day for one whole month before you step foot on a real runway. If that doesn't work, New Era isn't in need of your services. You're dismissed," Ines yelled.

"I sure hope so," Francois added.

———

We had the rest of the day off. It would be a good chance to learn more about modelling and walking the runway.

Zane was trying to be friends with everyone. He told us to come down to the lounge room in the basement where the boys all hang out.

"This is so cool." Jafari said when we got there. This place made the video clubs back home look amateurish. It could easily fit two hundred people inside and had the latest state of the art consoles and TVs with an open food section and bar.

"Don't just stand there." Jafari dragged me to one of the TV stations. Jafari kept trying to show me how to use the controller, but I couldn't get all of the buttons down.

"I give up. It's hopeless. I can't do this," I groaned,

sitting back on the couch. I was horrible at FIFA. Just want to taste the delicious food they had.

"Hey Abbasi, how was your audition?" Zane said joining us at our station.

"Could've been better, but I'm not complaining."

"Mines was the worst. I didn't do good today." Jafari said chiming in.

"It'll get better. It was the same with me when I first came here two months ago," Zane said staring at the screen while Jafari played.

"Thanks. That's good to know" Jafari replied. I can see that Zane was going to be in everyone's business.

"Enough about work. There's a party tonight at *Kilometre Zero*; the biggest club in town. Are ya'll up to go check it out?"

I thought he was joking especially on our first day after the runway episode.

"Hell, yeah we're up for it. Just tell me where." Jafari shouted jumping up. A part of me wanted to go, so I could see the nightlife of Paris and part of me didn't. Zane gave us the address and his phone number, in case we got lost.

After a few hours, we went back upstairs. Jafari kept annoying the hell out of me about what he should wear. I didn't care. "Should I wear the red or the grey one?" Jafari said holding up two shirts.

"They all look the same, just put one on." I said as I went into the bathroom. I put on a white polo shirt and jeans. This was the boys' common dress back home.

Jafari and I took a taxi downtown. Since Zane said it was the biggest club in Paris, my expectations were high. The Centre differed from where we were staying. It was packed; tourists, kids and everyone was outside. As we drove through, we passed by the Eiffel Tower. The view was breath-taking and Jafari was busy staring at women as the traffic began to thicken.

The driver stopped in the middle of a busy street after taking many turns. "That will be ten euros."

I paid and got out.

Jafari already started walking.

"So where is this place? Zane said it was in the centre. I don't know how we're supposed to find it."

"Just go straight." We pushed through the crowd, trying our best to stay together. Jafari ran out of patience and phoned Zane to meet us somewhere. He told us to wait for him in front of a café nearby. There were so many people on the street that I wondered whether they will ever go home.

"He's taking too damn long." I said, contemplating about asking someone.

"Be patient. It's Friday night. There a lot of traffic." Sounds like Jafari wants me to have patience now? What a coincidence! Judging Zane's cockiness, he seemed like the type who would be late to everything.

Moments later, Zane yelled from a distance. We

waved, seeing him. Jafari yelled almost causing my ears to deafen. This guy needs some manners.

Kilometre Zero was more than I expected it to be. I've been to a few clubs but this was awesome. The flashing lights and steam from the floor covered each corner of the venue. House music was blasting from the speakers while the dance floor was crowded. There were two floors; one for regulars and one for the VIPs.

Zane led us to one of the tables on the first where some of the boys from the cafeteria were sitting. Daniel was sitting in the middle of a couch with two beautiful French girls on each side of him.

Once they saw us, they cheered. I said what's up and Jafari ordered himself a drink.

"Don't get wasted. I'm not planning on dragging you back home." I whispered.

Jafari pretended like he didn't hear me and ordered a second after gulping down the first.

I was scared to loosen up. Zane ordered a bottle of Grand Marnier and poured me a glass. I took my time drinking it. For some reason, I had a feeling that the boys didn't party a lot. They were overdoing things.

Maybe this had something to do with the mentors controlling everything, from the time we came in and out of the building to our fitness reports. They wanted to know everything about you.

The guys got up and went to the dance floor with some bad chicks. Jafari started blushing when one of them grabbed him.

I laughed awkwardly and poured myself another glass. Time to reflect on the fun I had back home while waiting for someone to come up and grab me. Me and my friends would meet up at the railway station sometimes late at night and do crazy stuff. All stuff that we made sure our parents didn't find out about. I miss you Cameroon.

"Why are you sitting here all by yourself?" Daniel came back sweaty, plopping down on the couch.

"I'm cool. Just waiting for my turn." I said looking into the crowd. We laughed.

"Are you a fucking priest, Abbasi? Have some damn fun tonight."

I peeped Jafari on the dance floor having the time of his life, laughing loudly with the girl he was dancing with.

"Okay pour me another glass, bro. I'm almost ready."

Daniel pumped his fists, grabbing the bottle and filling my glass until it started spilling over.

"Fucking bloody cunt" I yelled out. The liquor was sweet like juice.

The three drinks I consumed, quickly turned into six. Oh my God! I'm feeling it now.

"Woah! Slow down there, buddy. We'll have to carry you home." Jafari now back, grabbing the seventh from my hands. I snatched it back. *Let me do me.*

Daniel and Zane were acting like a party animals along with the rest of the guys. They came back from the dance floor and drank more and more. I was so wasted; only seeing blurs of the DJ's booth and lights on the ceiling. I just kept laughing and laughing while falling and falling.

After a few more drinks, I was being dragged out by two guys who I couldn't see their faces. On the brink of blacking out, I heard them saying, *"We're going home. Abbasi's fucking wasted."*

Would my nights in Paris often wind up like this? I tried opening my eyes to look outside the taxi's window but they were too heavy. I hope I remember what happened in the morning.

2

CA ROULE?

HOW'S LIFE?

What's the deal with this big headache? *'Open your eyes'* my alarm kept going off. I was lying on the couch in the living room, with the same clothes on from last night. I felt like I was going to die.

I looked to the other side of the room and saw Jafari sleep on the floor. How could I let myself get so wasted? I was never the person who couldn't remember what he had done. What the hell happened last night? What if Ines and Francois had seen me? I griped, not believing what I'd gotten myself into. How could I be so stupid?

Zane wasn't no where to be found. I slowly got up, holding my head. This hangover would last all day and I wasn't so sure if I could go out today. Did these guys set me up? Who knows? I can only blame myself.

"Hey Jafari, do we have anything scheduled today?" I said trying to wake him up. He mumbled something and rolled over. No use. I headed to the bathroom to freshen up.

Do we have training today? I felt the urge to hurry. Jafari wouldn't budge, leaving me no choice but to pour water on him.

"What the hell!?" He jumped up, terrified.

"You had it coming. Now, hurry. We need to go to the hall to find out if we have training today." I fixed my clothes while waiting for him. He got dressed quickly, and we headed out.

"Why don't we call out today? I have a killer headache," he complained while making our way to the elevator.

"Not happening. I have one, too." I pressed the number for the first floor.

Once we got to the first floor, I noticed was there were more guys than last time. In all, about forty were present. The runway was the same as we left it, and there were only five chairs placed for the audience. I'm glad we weren't late, but I was nervous more about what we didn't know.

I noticed Zane coming with the rest of his crew, laughing together.

"I'm too tired for this, today." Jafari said lowering his head.

"I think we're all wasted."

"Seems like Francois and Ines are taking their time today." Zane said.

We waited for them for them for over an hour, chatting and drinking cups of coffee. Everyone thought that maybe the session was cancelled.

"Can we not do this today?" I thought.

Right when I was almost ready to leave out, a group of five women wearing fancy clothing entered the hall, looking around. Their age ranges were from 40s to 60s. Why were they here? Gracefully, they took seats in the front row of the main practice runway which was a few feet away.

"Well, that's a little weird, isn't it? Isn't it their third time coming in the last month?" I overheard a conversation behind me.

"Who are these women?" I thought.

"Hey, man. I heard you saying something. Do you know these women?"

"I think they are some millionaires here in Paris." The man stated.

"Their husbands must be filthy rich if they have time to watch us train." I chuckled sarcastically.

"I heard they might be the lead sponsors of New Era, not their husbands." Another man whispered.

I was in suspense until my name was called first. The crowd looked at me angrily because I didn't respond right straight away.

"Abbasi, wake up. Come up to the stage now." Francois said sarcastically while the boys in the crowd laughed.

I didn't notice Pauline, Francois and Ines had arrived and I quickly got up. The gazes from the five women were more intimidating than the crowd themselves. I looked seeing the group of women whispering to one another. The runway was mine for a solid minute and I was sure to leave a lasting impression. The DJ turned on the music and I was good to go. *Let's do this.*

Ines, Francois and Pauline seemed satisfied. My clothing stood out as a negative, but I knew once I made some money, I would upgrade.

"You're one of my favourites Abbasi, keep up the good work." I smiled at Ines. Her compliments weren't given away easily.

The reaction from most of the boys seemed positive but of course, there were haters like Zane. It was the same way back home when I was first joined the football team. My teammates were mad that the coach put me in the starting lineup instead of one of them. *It is what it is.*

———

Most of the boys hung around in the main hall for another hour, after the practice session, chatting just about everything.

The loud cries of hearing Francois and Ines yelling at some of the guys messing up was a sight to remember. It was funny to see them covering their faces and waving their hands; expressing displeasure. The five women who came were solely concentrated on us as if they were choosing whom they wanted for themselves. I have no idea why they were in attendance.

I expected Zane to come talk to me and Jafari about last night but he didn't. Was he embarrassed by me? I made a fool of myself and grew tired of thinking about it. Judging by the look on his face, it looked as something was troubling him during the practice session. I'll leave him alone and check in with him later.

Jafari almost fainted. I helped him back to the room and laid him on the couch. Somehow, he later ended up on the floor asleep. I didn't want to be stuck in the house, so I took a tour around New Era hoping to meet somebody.

I started off going to the cafeteria. I got a taste for a salad and some orange juice. After eating that burger the other day, I doubt if I would ever stuff myself again.

None of the guys looked welcoming, so I stood with my tray just looking around. Behold, there's a white guy in the corner smiling while playing on his phone. Maybe he's a good guy? What do I have to lose?

I walked slowly towards the table. "Hey, you mind if I sit here?"

He paused, looking up from his phone. "Nope, go ahead."

"Thank you."

"No problem, bro."

"Sorry to ask but how long have you been here?" I said hoping to start a good conversation. He put his phone down chuckling.

"For about a month now. I just got paid, so you know I'm happy." "What about you?"

"For three days."

The guy was gulping down his food as if he hadn't eaten in days. "Oh, so you're one of the new recruits. Good luck."

We laughed momentarily. "I would need luck for sure."

"Tell me. How have you lasted this long with Francois and Ines yelling at the top of their lungs?"

"I'm not that good, but I learned tips from others' mistakes. Honestly, God's grace helped me get by so far."

I nodded. The man wasn't attractive and had a bunch of tattoos. Does he have it? Only God knows best.

"Ines and Francois's been treating people like rubbish ever since I got here. No big deal."

"They must be famous models themselves? I haven't seen their faces in any magazines back home." I said it like I really know what I was talking about.

The man laughed as if he was a dungeon master. *So annoying!*

"Hell no. They're only employees here. Ines has a real short temper and Francois tries to act as if he's a perfectionist. The perfect duo I'd say. However, they're the real deal and have trained supermodels for different agencies for a few years. Now they're stuck with us."

"Ines told me I was one of her favourites earlier. Should I take it as a compliment?"

He shook his head. "She's sweet to the new models that she likes only. You must have caught her eye. It's hard to receive compliments in the modelling world. Consider yourself lucky she said that."

Finally, someone here I enjoying talking with.

"I'm Dimitri, by the way. I came all the way here from Russia and was recruited at a coffee shop where a lady named Anna visited often." He said in broken English.

I told him about my amateur football passion back in Cameroon but didn't tell him anything else. I kept Anna's name out of my mouth. What a coincidence!

A few minutes later, Dimitri had to prepare for a photoshoot. "Expect many of those to come" he told me as he was leaving.

"Hopefully?"

I got back to the room needing to use the bathroom from drinking so much water. Jafari had taken a shower, and the the floor was left wet. *What the hell is going on here?* My new pair of socks are soaked. God dammit!

I kept fuming as I went rummaging through my drawers, hoping to find another pair. *None.* I have no choice but to open Zane's drawer to borrow a pair from him. Hopefully, he wouldn't mind.

Combing through his drawer, I felt a plastic item and took it out and looked at it closely. *What the fuck, bro?*

———

It was a dildo. What was that thing doing in his drawer? He couldn't possibly use it on himself. My mind was wandering all over the place. *"Was Zane gay? Was he taking it up the ass?"* He didn't act like he was. Something else is going on here. Before he gets back, I have to put this thing back exactly where how it was. I closed the drawer, went to Jafari's and grabbed a pair of fresh socks instead.

Resting back on the headboard, my eyes couldn't stop looking at Zane's drawer. It was his thing, so why should I care?

Zane suddenly barged in the room, dropping his duffel bag on the bed. "Hey, what's up, Cameroon?"

"Yo, where have you been?"

"Around." He mumbled before going into the bathroom.

Thirty minutes passed and he still didn't come out. I had no right prying in his business but if he was sneaking around doing stupid shit, we could get in trouble as well.

Finally, Mr. Zane's out the bathroom; hair dripping and looking like a wet mess. He was in a rush, combing his slick black hair. Then, he put some fresh clothes inside his duffel bag.

"Are you going out again? Not sure what has gotten into him. Zane was acting funny and acted as if he didn't have any roommates.

"Me and Daniel are going to this bar with these hot chicks. Double date thing. You wouldn't get it."

This guy is lying up a storm. Why would someone bring a duffel bag to a bar for a date? Wherever he's going, he was spending the night out. Surprisingly, Zane never slept here once since I arrived. Jafari didn't care as long as he could watch TV undisturbed.

In a matter of minutes, Zane zipped out the door without saying goodbye. What's this guy up to? This Italian's a real freak.

Maybe I should follow him, but then again let me leave him to be. I'm thinking too hard about all of this. Meanwhile, Jafari was still sound asleep. I should go out and get some fresh air.

I went down to the building's library and saw a book I was interested in borrowing. Waiting in line made to start feeling homesick. There was a phone in the lobby but only for local calls. Oh yeah! I can call Mom on Viber. I opened the app on my phone and for the first time in almost a week, I spoke to my folks. They would be so happy to hear from me. Mom picked up the phone immediately and almost made me cry as I listened to her. I promised I'll be there soon. She told me that Dad was at work and him and Imani were doing okay since arriving to school.

A week had passed by since I discovered that dildo in Zane's drawer. He slept here probably a total of three nights. We just said what's up to each other while going in and out of the bathroom. It seems as if our room had became an airport restroom. Jafari didn't say anything but was hurt because he didn't know where to hang out.

"Are you even paying attention?" Jafari's voice snapped me out of my thoughts.

"Huh?" I turned, trying my best to act interested.

"We need to go to the lounge extra early today to get our seats in front of the large TV."

"Why, what's the big deal?" I don't know why we have to reserve our seats just to watch TV.

"Are you serious? It's the FIFA World Cup Finals, man."

I chuckled. "We should organise a game here, make our own teams, and go against one another. Do you even know how to play?"

"No, but that's beside the point but you're a professional footballer, right?"

I laughed at his sarcasm.

"Shouldn't you focus on walking down the runway?" I responded sarcastically.

"Okay, I'll find some good players. Our team would whip yours any day."

This conversation's hilarious. "You ready to go?"

———

For the past few days, Daniel wasn't around the building. I saw his crew wandering around acting like there was nothing to do. I wondered if Zane and Daniel were out together doing something illegal. There's only one way to find out.

Today we're having our first photoshoot and there

are more staff than usual; all swarming the building with racks of clothes, makeup kits, setting up lighting and practicing with the models. Ines's assistants handed out style patterns to each model with specific instructions.

Jafari and I were the last to get our fits and forced to hurry. The lines for the changing rooms were long; we waited close to fifteen minutes before going in.

The assistants then directed us to sit in the lounge and wait until being called. There were others who randomly came over and tutored us on the art of posing and how to get in our best positions. I still didn't know what the heck I was doing.

The clothes, we were wearing, were high-end. I was careful. Some sections of the outfits were tight around the arms and crouch. I felt weird wearing these skinny jeans and tight ass shirts.

Almost all the models were struggling with fitting into them as well. The photoshoot took longer than I expected and Zane still didn't come. Right before it was my turn to pose, Daniel came walking in, looking dumbfounded. His eyes were red and he appeared to be drunk. Was he? How could he risk getting fired? It's none of my business.

It was my turn and I walked calmly towards the set. "Abbasi, do your best and relax. You're the man." Francois told me.

"Okay" I shifted my weight to one leg, lowering me head and staring at the cameras. My facial expression was semi-serious, placing my hands in my pockets as I shifted from side to side. The photographers snapped away and seemed satisfied with the shots.

After fifty or something shots, one photographer said, "It looks like you're a natural, my friend." while still concentrating on adjusting his lenses.

"Ines, look out for this one. He has great potential."

"Merci." I responded.

"Oh, I know Victor. He's already one of our best gems here.

"One of the best already." Their words lifted my spirits. I remained seated after my turn, carefully watching others.

Ines after a few models had finished, came to my side, taking an empty seat. I respectfully turned away, hoping she'd gotten the message and would move away, but she didn't. Then, she said:

"I'm thinking about giving you some private lessons. What do you think?"

"Wow! I'm shocked. But can you say repeat what you said?"

"You heard me clearly, private lessons. Many of the newbies would kill to be in your shoes." I was afraid if I misunderstood her. Honestly, I didn't know what to say.

"Don't act so stiff. It's not like I'm going to kill you." She chuckled. "You'll have great opportunities in the future of New Era." Was she being honest? I had no way of knowing.

"Oh, sure." I said fidgeting. My gut feeling was to stay far away from her.

"I will be in touch with you with the details."

"Okay. Thanks."

Jafari was wrapping up and did better than I expected, impressing even Ines.

He couldn't contain himself, performing some dance moves. Everyone laughed, and then we went back upstairs to our room.

Is Zane upstairs? Who knows?

On our way to our room, Jafari kept talking about the compliments he received, still believing that maybe the people there were lying. I told him to chill out. I had more important business to deal with; how I was going to deal with Zane and his dildo.

There was no guarantee Zane would come in tonight. I couldn't relax. What else is he hiding? I purposely went through his drawers while Jafari was in the front playing FIFA. He borrowed a neighbor's Playstation for the day.

"What are you doing?" Jafari said looking confused.

"I lent Zane my damn charger and I need it."

He shrugged, believing me and turned back around. His attention was on the match he was playing online. That was all I needed.

Zane had three duffel bags and a suitcase. Man, he has a lot of clothes. A part of me believed Zane knew I found his dildo.

Maybe I misunderstood him? I came from Africa, and people didn't do that freaky shit back home. "Hey, man. He must have took it with him." I sighed, closing the last bag. There wasn't anything out of the ordinary inside of them.

For an hour, I sat back watching a Cameroonian talk show on my laptop before Zane barged in. Just as I was into the second episode - the one I was waiting for, Zane walked pass not even noticing us. This time, he was carrying a new bag.

"Hey, wassup?" Zane said trying to act like regular.

"Chilling, nothing much." My eyes were glued to my laptop, giving him a taste of his own medicine. He went to the bathroom and showered.

I put my shoes on and shut off the laptop. Zane didn't take long showering and when he finished, he got dress quickly. *Did he even wipe the water off his body?"* I wondered. Anyway, I started listening to some music and not once did he look at us.

Without a single word, he put on his coat and left out.

"What's with him?" Jafari yelled.

"Not a clue, I'll head down to the cafeteria. Want me to get you something?" I prayed he wouldn't want to come.

"Not really. You go ahead. I'm good."

Already wasting time talking to Jafari, I hurried out the door to the elevator. Was I making the right decision not respecting this man's privacy?

When I got to the first floor, I spotted Zane, walking towards the exit of the building. I made sure not to get caught trailing him. Zane didn't own a car, but why is he heading in the direction of the parking lot? I followed him, ducking behind a car close by.

I stepped on something causing a screech; making Zane turn around and look. What's he hiding? Zane walked faster and I had a full view of where he was heading. Then, a car door suddenly opened.

A driver stepped out of the vehicle and let Zane inside. Who else is inside? This is becoming dangerous. The driver walked a few steps away from the car to take a smoke. Out of my view, I took a few steps closer.

Now I was closer, I peeked to see if he was alone in the backseat. He wasn't. There was an older woman who appeared to be caressing his face. What's going on here?

Zane's face was between her hands, forcing him to look at her. He appeared to be unhappy about something. Once she saw he didn't want to talk, the woman forcefully pushed his face away, laughing and pulled out a cigarette rolling, down the window.

I saw her face and realized she was one of the five women who came to watch us when we practiced on the runway a few weeks back. Was Zane being forced into working as an escort? Maybe?

There wasn't a better explanation, and I finally got to see what was going on behind the scenes. Sexual exploitation of the models coming to the agency didn't seem farfetched. Zane was being boy-toyed.

A noise coming from a near distance caught my attention. The driver was approaching. I hid under the car as the driver passed by.

"I need to help Zane get out of this." I thought. I made it back to the stairs and before I went inside, I looked back to see if the car was still there.

It drove off screeching. Zane was standing alone, looking visibly frustrated. I hurried back upstairs, thinking on how I would talk to Zane.

Jafari wasn't at home when I got back. I opened a book while my sights was set on the front door. Minutes passed and Zane came inside, gently closing the door. My eyes kept stealing glances in his direction.

Would he say something?

"You're back so soon?"

"The cafeteria."

I wasn't going to play these games with him. I closed my book and placed it by my side. "Are you in some trouble, Zane?"

"What are you talking about, man?" He laughed while fixing his bed and then plopping down. He tried to ignore me, looking at his phone.

"Is someone forcing you to do something?"

Zane froze and only his eyes turned towards me.

"Why would you say that?"

He was panicking, but I wouldn't back down. "I saw you with that millionaire woman in the car, Zane."

"Were you fucking following me?"

"That's beside the point. What are you doing bro?"

"It's none of your damn business. Just continue reading your fucking book and stay out of my business or else."

This is getting ugly.

"What the fuck bro? I can't just ignore what I saw. I'm sorry, Zane." Zane began balling up his fists. "I couldn't care less if you want to fight because we can fight right here."

He back down saying, "I don't need your help, African. Do you understand me?"

"You're fucking lying. Just let me know what the fuck's going on. We can work together to deal with this shit.", I pleaded while approaching him, but he pushed me away.

"I don't need your fucking help. Stay away from me you god-damn freak." Zane then got up and left out.

Zane was dumb as shit. He could jam us all up if he got caught messing around with these sponsors.

Suddenly, I remembered that Ines sent me a text earlier to come up to her office at 8 p.m. for our first private lesson. Why the hell is it in the evening? Doesn't she have a life? I took a breath, checking the time; it was 7 o'clock. Thank goodness, I still have another hour to get ready.

3

"QUI VIVRA VERRA"

THE FUTURE WILL TELL

The private lessons were held on the fourth floor; the last in the building. The secretary instructed me to be on time, but I was confused. Why were they so strict for private trainings?

I knocked double-checking the number that the secretary gave me.

After waiting a minute, I was buzzed in by Ines. The room was small and I was silent remaining in one spot. It appeared that I was the only one there so far.

"A few more guys will be here shortly. Make yourself comfortable." She grinned. I sat down wondering "Who else was coming?"

After a few minutes, two guys entered the room. I recognised them from the runway but didn't formally meet them. They sat besides me. "Hi, we're Gregory and Leo."

"I'm Debasi. Nice to meet you." I stayed silent while we waiting for the others to show up.

Gregory and Leon kept on bickering about something while I followed Ines's movements.

"While we wait for the rest, I will hand you papers to begin signing." She said grabbing a folder off her desk.

"Here you go." Each one of us was handed some papers and a pen. The print was small and I didn't bother reading through them all. I just signed it and handed it right back.

"Are you not going to read it thoroughly, Debasi?"

"I don't want to waste any more time. I'd like to start as soon as possible."

She smiled grabbing the papers from my hands. It seemed suspicious that she didn't respond to my remark. Ines appeared to be all about business.

"Sign it Gregory and Leon, we don't have all day. We have work to do."

"So, what are we supposed to do now?" I wondered as no one else showed up like Ines said they would. She took the papers from Gregory and Leon and then walked towards a door in the back of the room and opened it, letting in who appeared to be the five women at the practice runway the other day.

The woman in the car with Zane the other night was among them. She was wearing a long red coat and sunglasses, giving us a wicked smile. I turned away from her creepy looks. Why are these women here?

With no power to contest, I was afraid of what might

happen next. Dad always warned me of being irresponsible and now it looks as if he might be right.

"Boys, you are one of the lucky ones. Congratulations. You have been our best models so far, so New Era will double your salaries, but there's one thing you need to do in exchange.

"Abide by our sponsors' wishes. You will be called anytime; day or night."

"This was what Zane's been doing." I thought listening closely to Ines. These women who only wanted us for their personal sexual fantasies. This is an absolute disgrace forcing us to be their boy toys.

"What if we said no?" I said not afraid of repercussions. They had no right to do this to us. We are not slaves.

"Actually, I possess your bodies due to you just signing and agreeing to be our new escorts."

We were shocked, causing Ines and the women to smile gracefully.

We have now been mercilessly handed us over to these old women as boy toys.

I never expected this and didn't know how to react. The others didn't say anything as if they agreed. This left me to fight for myself.

The papers were signed and now we are male escorts. I shut my eyes and cursed for not reading the contract thoroughly. How could I be so stupid? I couldn't say that they forced me to sign because they didn't. *Welcome to the real world!*

"All step forward, my darlings. Let the ladies see who they are having."

I refused at first only thinking about my family and how they would feel if they found out I was a male sex worker. They own our souls until our contracts were over.

"Now, Abbasi or you will have problems." Ines insisted.

With no hope, I stepped forward, looking down while the women gazed at me lustfully.

"Who would be the first to have this young man?" One of them spoke.

There was a long moment of silence before one of them spoke up.

"I will do us the honours." A woman said revealing her dress's slit.

"Introduce yourselves to the ladies," Ines commanded us, clearing her throat, signalling us to hurry.

"My name's Gregory Van Pelt from South Africa."

"I'm Leo Rodriguez from Spain."

"I'm Abbasi Ademola from Cameroon." I said it without passion.

All of the women were enough to be my mother. I lowered my head, feeling defeated while Gregory and Leo seemed content.

Only God knew what they would ask of us. I only know that I would fight until I am free.

4

N'IMPORTE QUOI!

WHATEVER!

"Which one should I choose? Come on bro." I rolled my eyes as I watched Jafari holding up three shirts. We were in the mall for far too long and I was tired of going inside every single store. Jafari was caught up trying to dress to impress only to look his best at New Era.

He knew nothing about my dilemma and I didn't plan on telling him anything. I didn't want this to happen to anybody. Those women were criminals.

"Get that one." I chose the ugliest one out of sarcasm. He didn't need to catch attention for his own safety. His face looked awkward.

"Are you kidding me? This colour is really awful."

"It looks really good on you, bro. You would believe someone who gets compliments all the time, right?" I pressed on until he bought the shirt. Finally, we leaving out.

Jafari paid and had the fattest grin delighted by what

he bought. The mall was crowded and on our way out; we stopped to get some coffee.

While waiting, I checked my phone for some messages. The waiter eventually came over and took our orders.

"Abbasi, be honest with me. What's wrong with Zane these days? He's been acting weird, man." Jafari might be on to us.

"No, why would you ask that?"

"I don't know man. I feel like something is going on that we don't know about."

"Here you go." The waiter came and set our cups on the table. I thanked him while Jafari kept looking at me, expecting I'd say something.

"His grandmother has been sick for two weeks now. I think it might be something serious." I knew he would believe me if I said that.

"I think you're might be right. But he hasn't said anything."

"You know Zane. He likes to keep him to himself. The man keeps skeletons in his closet for God's sake. You know?"

Jafari and I laughed; sharing moments so far of working at New Era while we headed back.

Three days passed since my boy-toy contract went into effect lasting an entire year. I didn't know how I would put up with this nonsense.

Jafari and I went to the market to buy some personals and took a taxi back. When the driver got to our building, we saw a crowd gathered at New Era's tennis court on the side. "Did someone forget to tell me there was a match today?" Jafari jumped out leaving me to pay the driver.

My smile faded once I remembered I'd be at Madame's house this evening. I had goose bumps thinking about it. The last three days I've been thinking about this moment and how I could escape. The staff at New Era were closely monitoring us. If I could run away, what would happen when I got to the airport with no money and passport. I gave New Era mines when I first arrived. *What a dickhead!*

Today, the security guard told us when Jafari and I were leaving that we needed a day pass from the security guard to go to the market. This is insane.

Anyway, New Era's contract for the models was six months but the contract by Ines stated a year. Who knows what the hell is going on?

Lying on my bed, I closed my eyes and let out a deep breath. I tried holding it in until Jafari came back but you know how that went. How could I keep this secret for six months? What if they didn't let me leave at all? *My Lord!*

Then the one who I was least expecting came back home. Zane, who was dressed up in a blue suit. I didn't notice I was lying on his bed.

"Sorry." I mumbled standing up and going to my own.

"So, I hear Ines recruited you. Congratulations, bro. You're going to make some big money."

Why did he care if she did,? Wasn't he the one who told me he didn't want to talk anymore?

"Yeah, she thinks I'm the best out of the new recruits." I said sarcastically although being the best didn't do me no favours.

"Welcome to the club. I knew they would select you. You don't have to put your act on in front of me."

"By the way, who told you?" I asked.

"Come on Abbasi, you're not the only one. There is a good number of guys here who are part of the business."

I gasped not knowing there were many others.

"Who's the model that been here the longest?"

"You don't want to know. Just keep your mouth shut, fuck these bitches and get paid. And don't try to pry into their affairs. I'm warning you." Without a single word more, he walked inside the bathroom and closed the door.

"I have a few more questions for you Zane. Don't go nowhere." I shouted. Then, I started banging on the door like a lunatic.

"Listen, man. Don't involve me into any of your shitty plans. I didn't like this at first, but they give me big tips. I'm talking about hundreds of dollars each night. Don't fuck this up for us, bro." Zane said as he came out the bathroom.

I couldn't believe this guy. "Zane, they 're sexually abusing us. How are you okay with that?"

"I know what's best for me and my family. You think

because I'm Italian that I have lots of money. Don't be fooled by the slick hair and looks, bro."

"I'm not…." I tried to say something before he said.

"Take care of yourself from now on. Oh, by the way, don't be asking around trying to find the first model. I'm sure nobody would have the heart to tell you anything. He might even be dead from what I heard." He put his headphones on trying his best to ignore me.

There's no use talking to him right now. He thinks I won't find out the truth but I will.

———

It's time for lunch, so I'm going down to the cafeteria. Jafari was still at the tennis court. I saw Daniel sitting with one guy involved in a deep conversation in Armenian, so I decided to go and sit with them.

They looked at me strangely as I sat down. "What's up"? They replied back and continued on with their conversation.

"Robert's getting so much money out of it. We have to find a way to get you in, too." Daniel said looking over at me. He caught me eavesdropping, but I quickly turned away.

"I even heard that they're giving these newcomers a chance." One guy said.

"Who? Ines. Man, don't worry I got you." Daniel replied back before finally turning his attention to me.

"Long time no see, Mr. Abbasi. What's going on with you these days?"

"How can I help you Daniel?" I never liked this guy. He was fake.

"Well, I'll be straightforward. How do I get on that woman's good side?" He was referring to Ines.

I chuckled. "You need to have skills, my brother. I thought you were already on her A-list. Are you losing it?"

"Things have spiralled out of control over the past few weeks."

His honesty didn't impress me.

"How do you expect me to help you? I'm a newcomer, remember." If I could help him, I could use him as an insider. He knew a lot about the agency.

"Teach my friend here how to be a better model, and I'll help you with anything you need."

"Agreed?"

"It's a deal. Let me start by telling you that Ines isn't that scary but you need to be pay attention to details. She's strict and wants you to mess up. Sometimes, she doesn't like to follow her own fucking rules."

The guy's face was stunned.

"I'll be in touch." I said walking away.

————

With Daniel in my pocket, I was a step closer to finding

out who was the first. I came back home to find Jafari on his bed. "How was the match?" I asked.

"They were all so bad. I thought I could join in for the doubles, but somehow all the teams were full. I signed up to play tomorrow."

Two weeks have passed since he last played. He was rusty but thought nobody could beat him.

"You need to come and watch me play tomorrow in a singles match. It'll be fun."

"I'll try my best." If I wasn't stuck at Madame's house, I would. Speaking of tonight, I need to come up with a lie quickly to tell Jafari.

How could I get dressed without him asking me where I was going? Jafari was playing on his phone, giving me some needed time to gather my thoughts.

"I'm going to this party tonight. Me and the rest of the guys in private lessons were the only ones invited, unfortunately."

Jafari appeared disappointed.

"Sorry." I mumbled. Jafari wouldn't be if only he knew where I was headed.

"Once I make it to the private lessons, I'll be right there with you."

"You'll get there, bro. Don't worry." I replied.

I took a long cold shower with no desire to turn off the water. The clock was ticking in and I knew I had to be there on time. I didn't care whether she like my appearance or not. I'm a sex slave.

"That was a long shower. Are you sure you won't be late?" Jafari said standing up.

"Oh no but I need to hurry. I wouldn't want to keep the boys waiting." Before I knew it, I was out the door, only carrying a backpack filled with personals. and fresh underwear. I was told that someone would pick me up in a black Range Rover in the building's parking lot. I waited in the main lobby looking out the front door and didn't see anyone except the security guard. The old man practically lives in this place.

Growing impatient by the minute, I was ready to go back upstairs when a car stopped in front of the building. It was the black Range Rover. The driver got out and walked to my side, opening the door for me.

"Bonsoir, you're Abbasi?" He asked.

"Oui." I said carefully before stepping inside.

The car's leather interior was smooth. I could sleep inside this vehicle all night. The driver closed my door gently and began to pull off. This was my first time inside a luxury vehicle and from my guess, it was the latest year's edition.

———

We were on our way to Madame's house roaming the streets of Paris. I had no desire to talk because I was so embarrassed. Soon enough, we were driving inside a gated community on Paris's outskirts.

The houses on the streets were all built flawlessly. The

driver informed me we were almost there. At that moment, I couldn't forgive myself for coming to France and falling for this scam.

The car turned onto a highway and five minutes later, we arrived at a mansion. The driver parked inside its driveway that could easily fit seven vehicles of its size. He then opened the door for me. Three glittering luxury sedans occupied the parking spaces as their gold rims seemed to reflect our presence.

Two maids were standing on the veranda and another who buzzed me inside. "The Madame has been waiting for you. Let me take your coat." she said.

"Merci."

The staircase diverged from the rest of the hall. It seamlessly matched with the décor of the house while the marble stairs matched had a delicate look. The Madame had an good taste despite her ugliness.

The maids and I walked towards the dining room where I saw Madame already eating at the end of the table. She was browsing on her phone while holding a glass of wine, tightly in her hand.

The maids stood by my side and after slowly taking the longest sip ever; she acknowledged my presence. Her eyes gleamed, and she put her phone down. "Abbasi, my amour. I'm so glad you made it!" She stood up, receiving me. I had a blank look on my face, irritated already.

"Come, have a seat." The maid pulled out a chair for me. I sat down and she ordered the maids to bring some food, pouring me a glass of wine. "What else would you like, my boy?" She said grinning.

"I'm good for now, Madame. Thank you."

Her stares pierced holes through my young soul. Was she infatuated by what we black men possess? Would she want me to do BDSM? My mind was all over the place.

"We'll have a lovely time together this evening, no need to look disappointed. Ines already told you, consider yourself one of the lucky ones."

"Oui, Madame." I responded half-heartedly.

For fifteen minutes, I remained silent while I ate and watched her watch me. She was captivated by my presence and tried making small talk, but I only had one-word answers. Right when I was finishing, Madame got up out of her seat, and came behind me, suddenly putting her hands on my chest and kissing my neck. I jerked uncomfortably and *now it begins.*

She grabbed me passionately; pulling me out of the chair and leading me up the staircase. Then, she opened a door revealing a master bedroom that was the double the size of my entire living room back home.

Once inside, I stood in the middle of the room and felt the door close gently. Madame came in front of me, pulling me towards her. I closed my eyes in disgust, the second her old lips met mine. So disgusting, but I was forced to go along. I kissed her back.

She broke the kiss and pushed me onto her bed, tenderly climbing on top of me. I turned my head to the side as she violently licked my neck. I noticed picture frames on the nightstand of what appeared to be her family. What if her husband knew what she was doing?

I clenched my fists, hoping this would be over quickly. She nibbled at my chest, getting rougher. "Relax," she mumbled, as I tensed. I couldn't enjoy having sex with this old woman. Would I be able to say no?

She returned her lips to mine and began reaching for my dick through my jeans. I felt so used. Still, I pretended I was into it.

Overwhelmed, I had to satisfy her and did so. Madame got tired quickly and wanted to stop after she climaxed. *What a quickie?* She was breathing heavily laying on my chest. I didn't move an inch, only putting my arm around her. She then fell asleep, snoring throughout the night. I tried pushing her off me but she kept grabbing. *What a waste!*

Madame's name is Katherine. She's married with three children. She felt miserable because her husband is always away on business. As we were fucking, she kept talking about everything including the bad sex life she had with him.

I caught myself chuckling at times but made sure not to offend. Madame was a deviant opportunist, exploiting us for her devilish desires.

The driver drove me back to New Era around eight in the morning, and for my first evening of work, Katherine paid me three hundred euros for twenty minutes of pleasure. I didn't even ejaculate. Honestly, I was ready to return her money but you know how it is.

"Have a good day," the driver remarked as I got out of the car. Thank God, I was back home. No one was in the hallways except the old security guard, who gave me a suspicious look, probably knowing already what had transpired overnight.

Beyond hunger, I needed to shower. No one was home, and then I remembered that Jafari had a tennis match today. I hurried as fast as I can as I planned on being there. Now, I'm ready to go, let's get some breakfast. Surprisingly, there was hardly anyone there. "Pancakes, beef bacon and orange juice, please." The order didn't take long and I was ready to eat.

Digging in, I looked around seeing two men of African descent coming inside who I never saw before. Are they visitors or new models? New Era told us that they only hired thirty guys this year. My guest was that they planned on letting some go soon. Maybe I should ask around.

The guys looked lost, just as me and Jafari when we first arrived. They stared around trying to guess where to sit. I watched them closely but tried hurrying up eating .

Shall I introduce myself? Nah. With only a few weeks passed by, I've learned that with modelling brings jealousy. You'll learn it's necessary to distance yourself as much as possible.

"Abbasi, I was looking everywhere for you." Daniel came in abruptly taking a seat by me. I was surprised he was up this early.

"You got something for me?" I replied.

Daniel almost choked, trying to answer.

"I… found out who was the first model here."

"Ok. Who is it?"

"It's a guy named Benjamin Rinaldi." He pulled out his phone, showing me his photo.

"I haven't seen him around here. Are you sure?"

"He left a year ago. I don't know why, but there were rumours going around that he was fucking Ines. Not sure if it's true or not."

"Do you know where I can find him?"

"Man, I don't know. But if you ask Trisha charmingly, I'm sure she'll give you his contact information."

"Should I?" I thought to myself remembering the looks she gave me and Jafari when we first arrived.

"I'm not sure about asking her but I'll think about it. Thank you, Daniel." I said smiling.

"You're welcome. Remember you promised to help get my guy in the private lessons, right?"

"Of course, no need to worry. I'm working on it."

He patted my back and left. I feel stuck in this never-ending cycle of getting up and going to these private sessions. In a few days, I'll get my first paycheck from New Era, and I'm looking forward to it. I'll probably send most of it home.

I got up and while exiting, the lunch lady gave me a enticing smile. Next stop: Jafari's tennis match. After that, I will be free for the rest of my day to start looking into Benjamin. How I would get this guy's contact? And if I did, what conversation could I strike when we first meet? There were so many things to consider.

———

Two hours had passed since I left Katherine's house and her taste was still in my mouth. *Yuck!* Once I got to the tennis court, I saw a large group of people sitting on the bleachers, eager for the match to start. I took a seat right on the top right seeing Jafari in plain sight.

He waved and I gave him a thumbs-up. I smiled, waving back. His opponent was warming up and acting friendly with Jafari. I know Jafari wanted to win this matchup badly. The whole agency was rooting for him and it would surely boost his morale.

The referee whistled, signalling the start of the match. Jafari got caught off guard and his opponent scored on the first serve. His opponent served again and Jafari quickly reacted. He struck the ball, backing his opponent close to the sideline. Then his opponent struck the ball faintly that it caught Jafari off guard again. 30-0.

"What the fuck, Jafari?" I yelled.

I couldn't believe Jafari was losing. He looked stressed now. I hope he will focus. Now, it was Jafari's turn to serve, and he took his time. He served and it didn't end up well.

His opponent was much faster than he was and he timed the ball precisely. He scored again. 45-0. Match Point.

"Come on, Jafari. You can do it!" Screaming out of my lungs, I was trying to give him all my support. I got a lot of looks, but who cares.

Jafari's opponent was caught off guard, playing too close to the net and Jafari used his strength to strike back. The ball passed went over his opponent's head, resulting in Jafari scoring his first points. 45-15.

Jafari hid his sigh of relief, but he really wanted to show it. After those first points, he appeared to get worse and his opponent went on to win the first two sets. Jafari would lose for sure. I gave up watching him, listening in on the guys' conversation next to me.

"He's such an amateur." One guy said as they laughed together at once. "Why is he even playing?" If Jafari heard the backstabbing going on in the stands, it would absolutely crush him.

"Why don't you guys go down there and let me see what you got?" I said, turning to them. All became silent too embarrassed to speak up, so they continued whispering to one another.

"Thought so." I yelled, standing up and leaving. After the match, I knew Jafari was having a temper tantrum in the changing area. I will go down and pay him a visit.

As I approached, I heard the sounds of crying. "Are you in here crying, bro? Seriously?" Once he saw me, he wiped his eyes and cleared his throat.

"How could I be so bad today?" Jafari said taking off his shirt and putting it in his backpack. I kept listening to him rant about this and that. "I can't understand how my form was off today. Coach kept telling me I was good, and now I have embarrassed myself in front of the whole agency."

"You are exaggerating. It was not as bad as you thought. You were just nervous."

"Not as bad? Come on, everyone in the stands were all laughing at me."

"You'll have a lot of time to practice. It's only our first month." With reps, Jafari could cement his reputation to be the best tennis player in New Era.

"Speaking of our first month, are we getting paid today or what?" Jafari said changing subjects. That made me smile.

"Probably, we should ask Human Resources since we don't have bank accounts yet. They will probably give us a check or something." Jafari's eyes lit up excited for his first payday.

"I have so many things I want to spend it on. You just don't know, bro."

"I think I'll give half to my family. Man, I need some new clothes." I replied.

"Me too, but I'm not giving them that much. Shit, I worked hard for this money." Jafari said chuckling. "I do want to buy a new phone." His phone's screen was cracked, and the colours on it were fading.

"What are you thinking about getting?"

"The latest iPhone."

"Yo, that's mad expensive. Come and let's get out of here." I stood up after he got dressed and we left. Jafari saw his opponent talking with the rest of the guys on the bench feeling cocky.

"Keep moving and don't say anything." I said pushing him in front of me.

———

The day after Jafari's horrible game, I planned my next move now that we got paid. I need to get Benjamin's address from Pauline's secretary, Trish. Perhaps, she would fall for my charm. If it meant sleeping with her, so be it.

I was walking around the bedroom, thinking of how I would approach the situation. Zane brought breakfast upstairs and surprisingly wanted to chat with me. I couldn't tell him about my plan.

"What's up with you, bro? You ain't saying anything."

"I'm a sex slave-a fucking boy toy for this agency. What else is there to say." I said blatantly.

"Hey, man there are some positives in this game. You get to fuck rich women every night. It's not as bad as you think. Give me your tips then." He said staring at his phone and finishing up his food.

"I don't understand how can you be so okay with this. Ines is using us."

"Abbasi, aren't you getting paid to fuck? I saw you last night getting into a Black Range Rover. It must have been your first appointment. Didn't you get a few hundreds of euros for your quality time? Imagine what you could make in six months, bro. With time, that lady may give you thousands euros to go shopping and etc."

"How do you know of all this? What's your role in it?"

"I was the same as you when I first started out two months ago. Actually, this is my third tour with New Era even before they became a modelling agency. Now, I make thousands per night. You got to be smart. You'll be finished before you know it and back in Cameroon as a rich man. Remember you're getting paid for two jobs not one."

"Do you really think what we are doing is right, Zane? This is some real bullshit."

Zane grabbed his plate and took mine away, leaving the area. I laid on the bed, stressed out, not believing what I was hearing.

All that Zane desired was money, looking good and dressing nicely. The women around the agency viewed him as cocky individual. He felt entitled to their immediate attention because he's been here probably the longest. I don't know how he could be satisfied being a boy toy. They probably knew what he was anyway.

I waited close to lunch to go to Trisha. She was nice but obeyed every order given by Pauline, Ines and Francois. I hope that my beaming smile sparks her attention.

The girl was Pauline's pet in reality. I avoided her when I could and now I have to get something from her. *Yikes.* I left, heading to the second floor, where her office was located. There were staff inside preparing for the next runway in the conference room a few doors down. Only the senior models like Zane were invited to partake.

I knocked on the door twice and received a welcoming, *"Come in."*

Trish turned her chair around, facing me. "May I help you?"

"Hmm. I just came by to see you. I was bored." I walked over to her bookshelf and pulling out one. "So, how many of these fantasies have you read by the way?"

"Not many. Most are new arrivals." She grabbed the book out of my hand and placed it back in its original place. "The reason for you coming here is…? And what was your name again?" I smiled following her back to her desk. "I'm Abbasi, and there are a few reasons why. The first being as I said that I'd like to get to know you." I said gripping the back of her chair. Her eyes widened, and then she slowly cracked a smile. *"Now I gotcha."* I thought.

Wasting no time, I went on to say, "Your beauty is immaculate. You're mixed with something, right? Maybe Cuban or Dominican." Trisha blushed, trying to hide it, but failed miserably.

"Italian my dear, and no I'm not mixed." She said avoiding looking at me and trying to act as if she was busy now.

"Italian, no wonder. They have the most beautiful women in the world. The first time I saw you I knew you were a model." She chuckled as her bright pink cheeks turned red.

"Abbasi, you are wasting your time and mine. Shouldn't you be preparing to train with Ines later today?"

"I'm free today. Are you free this evening for dinner?"

"Yes, I am and I have work to do. Can I really help you with something?"

"Answer one question for me and I'll leave you to be. When did you start working here?"

Trisha stuttered her words before talking. "I began here two years ago. That's my story." I sensed there was something more. Maybe she was an escort before she was hired. I faked being interested.

"That's wonderful. I wonder how Pauline was back then?"

"Much stricter I guess. She's the one who started New Era and is well respected in Europe's modelling industry." Now, it's time for me to ask the big questions.

"How much harder was it for the first models who worked here?"

"Not really hard, but most of them went on to bigger and better things once they finished with New Era. Some got recruited by bigger modelling agencies, some even in the United States. I suggest you take this seriously, Abbasi. Who knows, maybe you could be on the cover of Vogue someday?"

"So, it wasn't a single model, but a group?"

She sighed, visibly annoyed by my barrage of questions. "They were a group, yes. There was a guy named Benjamin, who was the best out of all of them."

I pondered how to ask her for his address and had a feeling she wouldn't give it to me unless I did something really special.

"Do you have the contact on Benjamin? Maybe I can pick his head for tips to help me and the other models around here."

She nodded. "Yes, we keep the models' records in those folders over there." I looked towards the direction she was directing. "We keep everything here and I mean everything. Now, that we have a new database, I have to enter all their information in it. Lord, this will take forever."

"I'm sorry. I could help you if you need it."

Then what I perceived as her moving to get Ben's information, her office phone rang.

"Hello?" she answered, nodding endless times and then hanging up. "Abbasi you need to leave. I have much work to do."

"My dear Trisha, I hope I didn't get you in trouble." I said while peeping her office keys on the edge of the desk.

"No, Abbasi, you didn't." Then, she bent down to grab something, and that's when I made off with her keys.

"See you later, Trisha. It was nice seeing you again." I was out the door, already planning my break-in for later tonight.

In the elevator, I stumbled upon Jafari, who was so

sweaty. "Where were you, you look like an alley cat?" I said holding my nose.

"Shut up. I was training."

I rolled my eyes, pushing the elevator button for the third floor. "Oh, I forgot to tell you. Ines was looking for you. I told her you was out but would be back shortly."

"Did she say anything else?"

"Hmm. That she needed to tell you something in private."

I took a quick shower and dressed. My phone buzzed with a message from Dad reading:

"Hello son, I hope things are going well. Me and your mother can't wait to see you, and your sister is off at university doing well. Call us when you get a chance. There are a few bills we need you to take care of. "

LOVE, DAD

I read it repeatedly. Their truthfulness is what I missed the most. Mom telling me to get up in the morning to drive Imani to work. I'm glad they're okay.

I replied:

"I'm OK, Dad. All is well. The good news is that I get paid in a few days. I'll send something. Don't worry. I'm doing okay and I'll see you soon." Sadly, I couldn't tell them the truth.

"Abbasi you need to go soon or Ines is going to be

pissed." Jafari stressed, and he was right. Ines had a terrible temper and I didn't want to be on her bad side. I headed to the elevators, expecting her to be on the last floor. "Come in!" She said hearing my loud bang. My ears could have gone deaf from her response.

"Finally," she muttered, gesturing at a seat in front of her. I sat and waited until she finished what she was doing.

"Katherine is very pleased with you. I'd like to congratulate you." She said smiling while her focus remained on her laptop.

"Congratulate me? Any man can please a woman. I feel ashamed that I was tricked into doing this." I said bluntly.

Angered at my response, she slammed her laptop shut, looking at me . "You better choose your words wisely from now on Abbasi. I will not tolerate this behaviour."

I said nothing nor apologised.

"Katherine wants to be with you again, so I scheduled you for tomorrow evening. What do you have to say now?" She said, crossing her arms.

"Am I supposed to? I just follow orders around her."

Again, I was being rude. Ines laughed, shaking her head. "It seems I need to teach you some lessons in manners as well." I didn't like her insulting me. Unfortunately, I wasn't in the position to challenge her. The best thing to do was to go along with it.

One positive out of the situation; I'm going to

Katherine's house tomorrow instead of tonight which would give me ample time to get Benjamin's information out of Trisha's office.

Ines lectured me for thirty minutes on ways to please Katherine and women in general. Honestly, her talking gave me a headache. I wanted to say "you can show by fucking me on this table", but she wasn't worth the time or day.

A text popped up on my phone from Jafari: *"Meet me and Zane at the lounge when you finish with Ines."* I came downstairs to see Jafari and Zane were playing FIFA. "Come and play, bro." They tried to teach me but I couldn't understand how to use the controls.

"Fucking cocksucker." Zane said after Jafari won. We laughed, as he was as bad as I was. At least, Zane knew how to play. "How can y'all be so bad at this game? This is the only game we play in Africa. I don't understand." Jafari bragged, earning a slap from Zane. I laughed so hard. It was now close to 5 p.m. and in an hour, the office officially closes. Trisha would have to leave her office door open because of her keys. For the remaining time, I played with them and once I figured out the controls, I almost won a few matches.

"Got to take a piss. I'll be back." I left Zane and Jafari bickering over a penalty. There wasn't anyone in the elevator and I proceeded to Trisha's office. I counted three cleaners in an office a few doors from the elevator and walked by without them seeing. Now at Trisha's office, I grabbed the knob and found the door was locked. I tried pulling it, but to no avail. Trisha found a way to lock it anyway.

I peeked behind in panic hearing the byes of some employees. Lowering my hood to avoid being seen, I picked the lock on the door and gently closed it behind me. The lights were off and I proceeded at the place where Trisha was pointing to earlier. There were so many boxes on the floor, it'll take me all night to find Benjamin's.

Every model seemed to have his own folder, inside of them were photos, bios and other information.

Finally, after shifting through one box, I got my hands on Benjamin Rinaldi's. I glanced at it, seeing pictures of his photo shoots, bio and newspaper articles. One paper had his full name, where he was born, and his address. "Yes!" I almost shouted.

I took pictures with my phone and placed it back in the box. All of the sudden, there were footsteps approaching. I hid behind the door and held my breath until they passed by. It was the workers

I slowly came out, locking the door behind me and hurried to the staircase. If the cameras spotted me, there would be repercussions for sure. Back in the room, Jafari and Zane weren't around. Now, I just need to come up with a plan to go see Benjamin Rinaldi.

5

ON N'EST PAS SORTI DE L'AUBERGE!

WE'RE NOT OUT OF THE WOODS YET!

I woke up extra early the next morning. Zane and Jafari were passed out, and I tried not waking them. I put on my shoes and grabbed my bag. There was an unsettling feeling in my stomach. Was I nervous? Surely. The thought of the lie I would tell the security guard when he asked. I'm sure he would report my leaving out early to the higher ups. I'd say I was going running.

"Bonjour Monsieur Abbasi, where are you headed so early this morning?" He asked firmly.

"On a quick jog. Probably to the supermarket afterwards." I said smiling back. The old man seems nice. He probably knew Benjamin Rinaldi. I think this guy has been working here his entire life. Goodbye and I was buzzed out. I walked for five minutes, then stopped in front of a coffee shop and saw a taxi parked. The driver was smoking a cigarette and looked as if he stayed up all night. "Is this taxi taken, sir?"

"Non." he responded.

I handed him the address and got inside. Meeting Benjamin will be a deal breaker on whether I would get out of this situation. Benjamin probably quit because he knew something fishy was going on. For some odd reason, I strongly believed so. Zane wouldn't have kept his name secret otherwise. I only hope that Benjamin could help.

We took many turns though the city and it felt like I was in the car most of the day. I was browsing and scrolling through Facebook and Instagram repeatedly, seeing Zane flaunt his new stuff he bought. He took a picture for everything. This guy surely loves attention and it was a turn off. I never knew what sort of satisfaction people got from being materialistic. Most of them aren't happy anyway.

———

We were now driving through Paris's suburbs passing through Mantes-La-Jolle and St. Denis. "*Mec,* these places are the roughest places in town.

"Reminds me of home." I replied.

The driver turned down the radio and replied back, "Don't go near these *quartiers* unless you want to lose your life." That made me laugh.

Fifteen minutes later, the driver announced, "Nous sommes *arrivés.*"

"*Merci bien.*"

I was outside a tall building; the facade resembled the ones built in the Victorian era. *What a fascinating sight!* Although it was classical, it didn't resemble a place where a popular model would live. I hope I got the address right.

"Did Trisha lie about Benjamin?" I'll reserve my opinion until I see him.

The door was open at the front entrance. I entered inside, looking on the first floor for Benjamin's place. *God dammit!* There's no elevator and by the looks of the building, each floor had at least fifty doors. When I got to the third floor, I found Benjamin's apartment at the end of the hallway. *Room thirty-four.* My heart was pounding heavily. I knocked on the old oak door a few times, until a white man in his late twenties opened it.

His appearance was sloppy and he had dark bags under his eyes. I can see that he hasn't been sleeping well. Honestly, he looked like a piece of shit, but his confused face was the only thing I focused on.

"May I help you?"

My sight shifted to his hand seeing he was holding a beer bottle.

"Are you Benjamin Rinaldi?" This guy wasn't anything Trisha described. He was the exact opposite.

"Yes. Is there a problem?" He said taking a long swig from the bottle.

"I really hope this guy doesn't want to fight." I thought to myself.

"My name's Abbasi. I came to ask you a few questions about the New Era modelling agency." His eyes scrunched at the name. Just when I felt like he was about to invite me inside, he slammed the door in my face. I was shocked and stood there for almost a minute. I knocked on the door again.

After a minute or two, he opened it with the most annoyed face. "What do you want pal? Are you one of their little puppets? Did they send you here to lure me back? Because if that's the case, I want to make something fucking clear." He grabbed the collar of my shirt and I raised my hands in defence.

"That's not the case. I'm a new model there and wanted to get some information from you that I can't ask anyone who's presently working there. Can you help me?"

He doesn't trust me, I get it. Thankfully, he released my collar and walked inside, leaving the door open. I didn't move when he said, "Don't stand there, come the fuck in."

The smell inside of his house was horrible. There was trash all over the place. The living room and the kitchen was messy. He escorted me to an old couch and sat on a broken chair in the far corner of the dim room.

Aside the clutter, it could have been a nice place before he moved in. Now, this wasn't an ideal situation for of a so-called supermodel. I had many questions and didn't know how to begin without being offensive.

"So, what do you want to know?" He took another swig from his bottle.

"I was recruited almost two months ago by a French lady who offered to pay for my ticket and living expenses. When I arrived, the first month was all fun and games besides the rigorous practices. Since then, things have spun out of control."

Benjamin chuckled. "It always starts out like that. You poor guys always fall for her kind words, promising you a better future and everything. When in reality, it's the exact opposite."

He shook his head. "Where did you get recruited?"

"It was at a football game in my country, Cameroon. I was finishing a match when this woman named Anna came up to me."

His eyes widened at the name. "She's a fucking snake, dude."

His words made me giggle.

"So, then she offered you this modelling job, and you agreed right away? Without knowing anything?"

"Yes." I said lowering my head, feeling ashamed.

"Never would I've guessed things would turn out like this. For all, I knew I thought I'd be helping my family by having a good job. Since I arrived, I've lied to my parents about my well-being. Forever, will I be a big disappointment!"

"There is no need to despair, but I will be straightforward with you. It was a foolish choice. We all make them.

Sure, you didn't know, but you needed to do your research first before accepting the offer. It's too late now." His words devastated me. It felt like I was being hit in the face.

"Now, I'm in another contract which forces me to do sexual favours for any woman, the agency requires."

Benjamin just looked and didn't express no remorse. I paused, wondering if he already knew this already.

"Go on," he demanded.

"A lady named Ines forced me into it. It was in the terms of a contract for a professional model training course. When I signed the dotted line, Ines declared that I was a boy toy by signing."

He nodded, looking down at his bottle. Deeply thinking, I tried cutting off his thoughts by pleading.

"Please tell me everything you know about New Era. I need to know, so I can expose them for who they are. I want to go home. I'll do anything."

———

Benjamin wasn't much of a talker. Judging from by his appearance, he was definitely in bad shape. Was it because of his past dealings with New Era?

He didn't answer me right away. We sat in silence for a few minutes. Then, he spoke. "You sound really desperate. If I tell you some information, you'll need to find proof and coordinate with the police. That's all I can do for you." He took a long pause and then continued, "That fucking place dude needs to be closed down forever."

His words were sincere but he didn't want to get his hands dirty. I'd be left alone to bear this if all fails. The thought of being a boy toy for the rest of my life scared me to death.

Suddenly, Benjamin came over to the couch, detailing what he knew to the best of his knowledge. As he was speaking, I could only shake my head in disbelief.

"I promise you I'll try my best to bring these mother-fuckers down." I exclaimed.

There was no choice. I'm forced to fight for my freedom and others caught up in this web of lies and deceit. I only hope the boys will be there to fight along-side me.

Benjamin handed me a bottle of Saint Sylvestre 3 Monts. I initially turned it down but wound up guzzling down half. *Damn, that shit got me feeling buzz already.* He started off by saying:

"I was just like you when I first started out. I had a job here at a local supermarket for almost a year. I moved here with a friend from Norway."

"One day that woman Anna, came to buy groceries and flirted with me. Then she came to shop almost every single day. Sometimes, twice a day. She flirted a lot, grabbing my arm and stuff, but I wasn't interested. I remember one day when I was

finished work and leaving, Anna was waiting for me outside, trying to offer me this job I knew nothing about."

"Modelling, of course." Benjamin chuckled. "She gave me her card and number. When I told my friend, he kept pressuring me to take the job because we were in so much debt because of the rent. I had no choice but to."

I nodded, listening closely.

"I ended up agreeing, only to find out I was the first model hired by New Era. They didn't know what they were doing at first. The agency found somehow to pay me. I can't lie, within six months I gained fame and made the agency some good money. When I wanted to leave after nine months, they told me I was in a contract for two years. I didn't read the contract thoroughly. I was blackmailed to pay back the money I earned and was forced to prostitute for the rest of the contract."

Somehow, his words didn't surprise me. We're in the same situation. He continued on:

"I found out Anna was a well-known scammer here in Paris. Pauline the CEO, has been running a human trafficking network for years. You could say this is her second job. But for New Era to last, they've had to bring in some rich donors. The five women, you met at the audition, have been around for a while. I know everything about them."

Chills started running up my spine. It was too much to take in all at once. I was getting mixed up in these dangerous peoples' affairs.

"Why haven't they been arrested? Don't the police know about this?"

"Don't be so naïve. The millionaires have all the power in France and in such cases, money blinds the court system, with the police being the first on their payrolls."

It'll be harder than I thought to expose the truth. I couldn't trust anyone at New Era. We finally agreed to proceed onwards and promised to help me all he could.

Benjamin was forced to work at East Side Burgers, a popular fast-food restaurant in Paris after his ordeal. Unfortunately, he was exposed as a sex worker after an undercover police sting and his face was all over the news. He didn't have the muscle, money or power to go up against the accusations. He ended up suing New Era in court and settling out for a few thousand euros. Nowadays, he is satisfied with any job that comes his way.

"Do you plan on leaving this country, starting all over?" I asked.

"Oui, but I don't have enough money saved up. My roommate left to pay for this shithole and I barely have anything left over at the end of the month. I'm getting there though."

If we could sue the agency, maybe it would bring some financial relief for all of us. Although, we had little chance of winning the case as of now, if we had enough evidence, we can take them down and get paid.

"That's good to know. I need to get back, but we'll be in touch." I gave Benjamin my number along with my email address. I felt vindicated knowing I wasn't alone. Out the door, I caught a taxi back to New Era.

———

On my way back, the only thing I could think about was getting back home. When I arrived, the unfortunate had taken place.

"Upstairs now, Monsieur Abbasi." Ines scolded me from the lobby to her office. She knew about me going out. "What makes you think you have the freedom to go out wherever and whenever you please?" She was furious, but I kept my composure, pretending to be apologetic. Jafari must have told her I left. Zane always kept his mouth shut and minded his own business. That was the one thing I liked about him.

"It will not happen again. I promise." I said rolling my eyes, which made her angrier.

"Oh, I know it won't because from now on you're not allowed to leave this building without my permission."

"Being imprisoned is not part of the contract, Madame."

"Thank you for reminding me, I'll make sure to add that in this evening." She smiled sarcastically. How could it be possible for her to annoy me so much? I didn't say a word after that.

"Now get yourself together and be at Katherine's place in two hours." I got up from the chair and left the room quickly.

Jafari would pay dearly for this. How could he be so stupid to report I was away? When I got back to the room, I burst through the door to find him playing on his phone.

"For someone who doesn't know how to be a professional model, you sure have a lot to say. Don't you?" I stood above him, my eyes glaring in anger.

"What do you mean? Where were you anyway?"

"Why did you tell Ines I was out?"

"I was worried, you were gone for a long time. She came by looking for you. What was I supposed to do?"

"Certainly, not tell her. Listen, just don't worry about me babysitting me, okay?" It wasn't his fault but I needed to protect him.

"So, if you went missing that's none of my business, right?"

"Exactly."

He knew he couldn't argue with me and win, so he went back to what he was doing. If he reports me to Ines again, he would see the worst in me.

With a little less than two hours remaining before going to Katherine's, I sat and pondered on what I needed to do for the evening. I should be thinking - What can I do for her to get rid of me? Be sweaty, unshaven, dirty, uninterested. I thought of many things, but knew she wouldn't fall for it. The woman told everything to Ines and probably had notes on me.

———

Zane came back from working out. He and Jafari talked about a photoshoot for tomorrow. I sat listening but not really paying attention.

"I heard a few rich ladies are going to be there. You better make a good impression." Immediately, I looked at Zane. He was trying to set Jafari up. I couldn't let that happen.

"Do you think they are really rich man? I heard they were old and beat-up." I said giggling.

Zane was amused but Jafari wasn't. "Nobody asked you, bro. Go on Zane." This guy is so obnoxious.

"As I was saying before we were rudely intruded upon, I'll talk to Ines, so she can know of your interest in private lessons."

"That's not happening. You're a damn clown, Zane." Jafari did not know what he would be getting himself into.

"You have no right to get in my business, Abbasi. One more fucking time and I…" Zane snapped, causing me to almost fight him.

"Hey, hey, hey. Chill out guys. It's not that serious." Jafari interjected.

"Fine." I said getting up. It was time for me to get

ready for Katherine. "But remember, when things get out of hand, don't come calling me." I left them with that.

———

The same driver in the **Black Range Rover** waited for me once again in the parking lot. I greeted him and entered the vehicle. *Let's get this shit over with!* The same maids were waiting for me at the gate and escorted me to Katherine's living room.

"Abbasi, I'm glad you made it back, ma chéri." Katherine said smiling.

"The pleasure's mine, Madame." She offered me a glass of wine and instructed me to sit. During our conversation, she placed her hand on my cock and met her lips on mine. I was caught off guard, so I slowly caressed her hair, pulling her head downwards.

The situation got more intense; her hands traveled down my chest, unbuttoning my shirt and unraveling my belt.

"Patience, Kat." I grinned, which she liked to my surprise.

I was now standing above her, putting my cock down her throat. This experience differed from the first time; I was more into it for some odd reason. Katherine sucked and slobbered it, almost choking. She gasped when my hand went up her dress revealing her red lace panties. I finger-fucked her until she climaxed like three times. My hands were so wet and Katherine was in heap of endless pants. After twenty minutes, I came in her mouth and she licked and swallowed every bit of it.

"You are so wonderful, my boy."

We laughed together. I felt relieved. If I could please her like this all the time without having to put it inside of her, Ines wouldn't bother me again. Or maybe?

Katherine got up and left the living room for the bathroom, leaving me alone. I wanted to see what I could find on her while she was gone.

Her house was gigantic and there were so many paintings on the walls. They all seemed to be from famous artists. I went upstairs to the second floor and almost got lost in a random room that appeared to belong to a teenager. There were framed portraits of a girl; a few years younger than I. Perhaps, this was her daughter.

Suddenly, I felt disgusted again. What the hell was I doing here? *Oh shit, I hear her calling my name.* I ignored hoping that this would be the excuse I needed to get kicked out.

"You shouldn't be up here, my dear," one of her maids said spotting me. I came downstairs only to be greeted by the same girl in the portraits upstairs.

"I told you. I do not want any workers on the second floor except you, Amanda." The girl was rude and passed by me rolling her eyes. She thought I was the help. *Yeah, right.* A minute later, Katherine came running towards the stairs terrified.

"Lora, I see you already met Abbasi. He's one of the new gardeners."

"Whatever, Mom." Lora said rushing to her room. Then, there was a loud slam from closing her door.

"Abbasi, you need to leave right now. The driver's waiting for you outside." Katherine pushed me towards the exit, handed me a check for 500 euros and shutting the door.

"Can I take a bath first?" were my initial thoughts.

The driver was ready and as usual dropped me off at the same spot. Once inside, I noticed Pauline giving a talk to a group of models in the lobby.

"It's official. They will be coming later this evening, so put on your best suits and come down to the party in the lobby around 10. This group of potential sponsors will be working with us for a very long time. Make them feel welcome and good luck."

I was puzzled. Who's she talking about? I went over to one guy to inquiry.

"What did Pauline just say? I missed it."

"There are an A-list agency that will be collaborating with New Era. To celebrate, there will be a welcoming party tonight."

What sort of scam were they masking behind this collaboration?

I saw Jafari and Zane standing together. They didn't see me while Pauline was talking. When they saw me, they acted like I didn't exist.

"So, are we going to the party tonight or what?" I said pretending as if nothing happened earlier.

"Me and Zane are going. Maybe not with you." I couldn't believe what he was saying.

"Oh, come on, you need to stop taking things out of context." I came between them, grabbing them tightly by their necks. Jafari winced and Zane tried pushing me away.

Zane seems to be turning Jafari against me and I didn't like it at all.

"I'm not but you need to chill sometimes, Abbasi. Trying to act like my father. I can take care of myself." Jafari softened his tone sounding as if he pardoned me. There wasn't anything to pardon for.

"I need to make a good impression for these rich people tonight. It feels like my last chance." Jafari sounded stressed.

"I'll help you, my brother. Don't worry about anything." Zane smiled crookedly.

"No, let me do the honours. It's the only way for me to show you how sorry I am."

"No, thanks. I don't need both of your help. I'll figure this out myself one way or another."

"Come on now, would you rather take advice from one of the best models around here, or stick to just being a pinup?" I pointed at Zane and he didn't find my words amusing.

———

Our room was a complete mess. Clothes were thrown everywhere and shoes were laying all around. Jafari had a lot of his clothes inside my closet space. *This guy's something else.* Should I wear something appropriate for the evening? Honestly, I don't care. Ines already controls me in her private network of sex trafficking. Just call me one of the *boy toys in Paris.*

Suddenly, I started thinking about Katherine and her relationship with her daughter. The girl seemed tired of her mother. I wonder if her father knew Katherine was having these promiscuous relationships. Maybe she's hiding it from both of them. Who cares, really?

I didn't want to have any relationship with her daughter. My secret with her mother would crush her if she found out.

"So, what should I wear, expert?" Jafari said snapping me out my dreams. He was holding up two suits; both which looked nice and classy.

"I think you should go with the black one."

He nodded and then went inside the bathroom to change. While I waited for him, my phone buzzed signaling a text.

From an unknown number, it read:

Pauline has the contracts she made with the five women millionaires you said keep showing up to your rehearsals; they are in her office somewhere. You need to find them, soon. Don't get caught.

—Benjamin

I looked up to see if Jafari was out of the bath-room; he was still inside. Once more, I carefully read the message. This could be a deal breaker if I found where they were. The time I went to Pauline's office, I remember seeing a bunch of cabinets with keypads. It would be absurd to get inside of the office undetected, let alone find the passwords for the cabinets.

"When will security be the least on guard upstairs?" I pondered. Maybe during the party.

I smiled to myself and yelled. "Hey, Jafari. Do you know if everyone in the building is going to the party?"

He yelled back, "Didn't you hear Pauline? It's a big thing."

"Great to know." I yelled back.

Let's throw on the best suit and get ready for the occasion.

"Yo, Jafari. Hurry up man. I need to get in the bathroom."

An hour passed and I was smelling good and looking good.

Our third-floor hallway was mobbed; everyone was eager to go down to the party. Some wore white tuxedos and others like myself dressed in all black. I stood around outside our door waiting for Jafari, who went to the bathroom to take a last-minute shit. After ten minutes; we went downstairs to the lobby.

Zane, Daniel and the rest of the guys showed up in style, some even started drinking already. Were they allowed to drink in front of guests? I don't know. It was none of my business. Speaking of Ines, where is the hell is she? Trisha, on the other hand, was creeping around, checking out our appearances.

"Are we going to stand here all by ourselves?" Jafari said as the music was blasting and the guests were now starting to come inside.

"You said you wanted to make a good impression. You won't, blending in with the regulars. Those guys over there are just came to show off. Look at that guy over there. He's wearing shorts and suit jacket."

We laughed so hard that I had to hold my stomach in.

"This is so big. Just look at the people in here already. High rollers with big money" Jafari said.

"It's not. Just wait, and then I'll tell you what to do." I responded, getting champagne from the waiter who had walked by.

"I can take care of myself. I'm not dumb, father."

This guy gets offended by anything I say. I left the rest of my drink on the table and walked around with Jafari. This boy is getting on my nerves.

"There's nothing to be nervous about, bro. Calm down. You're sweating bullets."

"Easy for you to say. You got it all." I felt bad for not

telling him what I know. Once he finds out, he would freak out for sure.

"Abbasi, look." I turned towards the front entrance. The special guests came in. Pauline was accompanying them and Ines and Francois were by her side.

"What should I do now?" Jafari exclaimed.

"Calm down, first and then take a few deep breaths. When one of them is alone, offer them a drink. Since all of them are women, aim for the one who has the most graceful look of elegance." Sipping my drink, I was checking out the VIPs.

They were laughing at something Pauline was saying. Her ego was on overdrive for sure tonight.

"What are they taking so long?" I shrugged in response. Pauline was probably setting the tone. Landing a deal with New Era would be like working for the devil. They knew nothing about what was really going on. It's a big scam.

Once Ines, Francois and Pauline left the guests to mingle, I nudged Jafari. He was ready and I wished him luck.

I watched closely, gingerly approaching a group. He began talking and surprisingly; they were all smiling.

"Don't fuck this up." I mumbled. Jafari called the waiter over and ordered them drinks. He gave me thumbs-up, signalling he was okay.

As I was observing him, Ines cut me out of my peaceful state and stood next to me. "You were at the brink of disaster early this evening. Be careful from now on." She warned.

"Well, what did you want me to do? Jump from the window?" She knew everything since she was in regular contact with Katherine.

"No, you had no business being on the second floor. You go where Katherine tells you to be only. You know what that means, right?"

"Yes, Madame."

"We'll let the situation die down for a bit. Until so, you will assigned to a different woman."

I groaned, as if I already knew. "Not a surprise."

"Don't get smart with me. I'll tell you more about it tomorrow. Oh, and while you're at it, have fun tonight." She clinked her glass with mine and walked back over to Pauline. My attention returned to Jafari, who was deeply engaged with one lady. *"Don't fuck her yet, bro"* I said to myself.

———

Ines and Pauline were having a long conversation probably about my incident at Katherine's. This is the perfect time to make my move. I exited the lobby, heading to the stairway and up to the fourth floor.

Gratefully, no was in the corridor. I began picking the lock. This time it took longer than Trisha's and every time I heard what I thought to be sounds, I panicked. After a few more tries, I was able to get it open. *Geesh!*

I went over to Pauline's desk to turn on her computer. *Damnit, it needs a password.* Why did I expect this to be easy?

I dropped down to open the drawers on the sides but they wouldn't budge. They were locked as well. I groaned, feeling vexed. There was no way I could open those drawers without the keys.

Suddenly, I heard someone talking outside. Then, the doorknob was turning. I hurried; hiding under a desk in the far back of the room.

The door then opened, and I can hear Pauline talking to another woman, most likely Ines.

"I wouldn't have bothered to throw this party if it wasn't for these dumb ass new sponsors. We are already up to our necks in debt. I don't know what to do." She whispered.

"Wow, New Era's in debt." I thought to myself.

"These femmes are paying less money for our escort services these days. They'll make us bankrupt, Ines."

"We need to start reducing the salaries of the new models and making them pay rent here. They're getting paid too much money. Most of them are not even good enough to walk in Tati." Ines said jokingly.

They laughed while I held my breath, hoping to avoid detection.

Seriously, cutting the models' salaries and making them pay rent? That's truly unfair! We're already over-worked and underpaid. I listened on.

"If we cut their salaries and make them pay rent,

after they've signed the contracts, they may all decide to leave. This means that we'll have to send Anna to recruit heavily again in a few months." Pauline seemed worried.

"You know what we can do. I have an idea, Pauline. We can look at selling their contracts to other agencies. They're our properties anyway."

Did I just hear Ines correctly? I knew what she was implying.

"I'm not your damn slave." My thoughts after her words.

Pauline paused and then snickered sounding like a horse. "How much do you think we can get for each model?"

This woman's a monster.

"Maybe twenty-five thousand Euros at least if we sell the buyers on their upsides. My advice is that we only sell the bad ones," Ines commented.

I must warn them before they become trafficked.

"Then there it is, my lovely assistant. Let's start with the bad ones. I'll be waiting for your report in the following days." Ines agreed.

"À votre santé."

"À la vôtre."

They clinged their glasses and left the office. I remained underneath the desk; terrified to exit.

————

Twenty minutes passed, and I returned downstairs to the

party. My face was drenched with sorrow. I had to tell Jafari, knowing he would might be one of the first ones for their plan. What if something happened to him?

I started looking around for Jafari in the crowd but didn't see him where I left him. I circled and still no Jafari. Let me go up to our room, maybe he had to use the bathroom again.

Oh, shit! He was having sex with a blonde. *Camera time!* As I inched closer, I saw it was one of Pauline's new sponsors. *Damn, this guy really fucked up now or did he?*

"Jafari, we need to talk right now. What the hell!" He shoved the lady off him, startled by my voice. His voice mumbled, 'What the fuck, bro?' The girl covered herself with the blankets and started grabbing for her clothes.

"Sorry, Sarah, can we take a break just for a few minutes? My Papa here needs to talk to me about something important."

Sarah snatched her purse and left the room, embarrassed.

"What the fuck is this all about, Papa?" He yelled.

"Where should I begin?" He would be so mad I didn't tell him sooner.

"Listen, don't freak out. There's something serious I have to tell you." Jafari usually overreacted to everything.

"Okay, go on. I have some good pussy to get back to."

I cleared my throat. "There are a lot of things you don't know about New Era. When we got hired, I thought it was the dream job, but certain things are happening beyond our control. I'm now dealing with bigger issues."

Jafari looked at me strangely.

"What are you saying, man? You're gay or something? I didn't know you…" This guy ain't taking me seriously.

"Hell no. What I'm trying to say is, New Era has forced me to be as a male escort." I felt so embarrassed. What would he think of me now?

"Yeah nice try, I'm too busy for this rubbish, Abbasi." He thought I was joking, but the second he saw I wasn't, he recollected himself.

"Are you fucking kidding me, bro?" He said as his brown eyes fixed on my lips without flickering.

"Ines deceived me. The private class she always talk about is not as such. You'll be forced to do sexual favours to women like the five old hags who showed up to our practices. You remember the women right?"

Jafari then realised why they were there for practices.

"They've been paying New Era for us guys from all over the world to be escorts. They only take a few to preserve the mystique. Everything's a secret. You must fuck them and do whatever they say. In exchange, they tip you."

"While you were away in your rendezvous, I sneaked inside Pauline's office." I continued.

"What? What were you doing there?"

"Not too loud. I was there to find contracts she made

with those women. They're somewhere locked in her cabinets." As I explained, Jafari was biting his fingernails visibly shaken.

"Jafari, I overheard something that's even more disturbing, bro." "They will began taking the models they see as amateurs and sell them to other agencies for the rest of their contracts. New Era's running out of money."

"What are we going to do? We need to go to the police!" Jafari's voice raised.

"Listen, we need to tell the others but not yet. The police are in the pockets of New Era and will not do anything. It's not as simple as you think."

Jafari already knew he was one of the amateurs.

"What the hell I'm going to do?"

"First, you need to get in good with that girl you were just fucking. You can blackmail her into helping you out. I got the video just in case she doesn't give in." I had to be honest with him without providing him with details.

"You fucker. I knew you were up to something."

"These new sponsors probably don't know about these escort services yet. If you fucked that girl that easily, for sure, they don't know what the hell's going on. Once the truth comes out, we'll all be free."

"Ok, I'll keep fucking the shit out of Sarah until you tell me what's next. But in the meantime…"

"Keep your cool and use your charm. You got some making up to do."

"At least, you got a card to play with to get out of this

shit. I'm still working on others." I said, reassuring Jafari everything will be okay.

––––––––

The next morning after the party, I went to sit out front at the entrance. Ines had text me to show up to her office at 9 AM sharp. *That's not happening this morning.* For most of the night I thought about how I would reveal the truth to the boys, but didn't have any suggestions. I could make flyers, putting them under every door. What if they took it as a prank? What if I got caught?

It's 9:15, and now I'm on my way to her office. As usual, she was reading in the newspaper not doing anything, when I entered. I took a seat, waiting for her to speak.

"Abbasi, you're late, as usual."

"Do you think I give a fuck?" I said to myself.

"Tell me something I don't know. Cut to the chase." Visiting her office wasn't something I was looking forward to.

"New Era's currently in a bad situation."

My thoughts on what she said. *"Of course, you are. Using models to do sex services instead of helping them launch their careers."*

"What does that have to do with me, Ines?"

"Well, we think you can be the one to help us. I've arranged a meeting with the next madame. She's agreed to pay five thousand euros. Two thirds of it, would go to us for our little, of course."

"First, you forced me into doing sexual acts; and now you want to shake me down? I don't understand you people. Aren't you already getting paid by them?"

"That's not your concern but for now on, you just work for us. I'm expecting you to abide by my orders." She replied nicely. Of course, I wasn't fooled.

"When's this meeting taking place and where?" I asked wanting to leave her office soon as possible.

"Since your little incident with Katherine, we've chosen another location for your services; a five-star hotel in Centre Ville de Paris. I will email you the information. It's will be this evening. Don't disappoint us or else."

I felt so used.

"That's all. You're dismissed." She said turning around and returning to read her newspaper. *This woman annoys the hell out of me. Who are her other foot soldiers besides Zane and Daniel?*

———

Down at the lounge, I found Jafari, laying down on the couch and Zane chilling besides him. They were talking about something when I came up. By the look on Jafari's face, he seemed worried.

"What's up with you?" The area was crowded, and a lot of talking in the background.

"Zane's sharing his thoughts on the situation, but I'm not sure if it would work."

"What the fuck? This was between us, bro. What sort of advice can Zane offer?"

"Calm down, Cameroon. I think Jafari should run away," Zane replied as he turned on the PlayStation.

"If it was that easy, wouldn't we all do the same, right?" Zane was pushing my buttons. Jafari is hard-headed.

"They'll find you in a heartbeat and sue your ass for breaking the contract. You'll be in Paris for the rest of your life paying them back."

Jafari looked disgusted. Pausing for a moment, he then responded, "You're right, bro. By the way, that girl from last night won't answer my phone calls. I think you fucked that up."

"We'll get her, no worries. Somebody here know who she is." I tried sounding convincing as possible.

"Do we say anything to the others, Zane?"

He shrugged his shoulders. "I don't care. It's their damn problem." *Why did I even bother asking him?*

"Come on and say something." I pleaded.

"I really don't know. Maybe get a group of the guys together and make the announcement? Once they hear us, they can decide what to do next." As much as I hated to admit it, Zane had a good idea.

"We could use our room as the meeting place later when the staff leaves."

"I can't do it. Ines got me meeting another Madame at a hotel downtown tonight."

Jafari looked at me while Zane snickered.

"Maybe before I leave. We need to put together a plan."

This will be tricky. Would they got to Ines and Francois the first chance they got? Or would they join us in bringing down New Era for good? Zane promised to help while Jafari said he'll buy the refreshments.

Back home, I started cleaning up, thinking about how I would present the scenario. For sure, some wouldn't believe me. Honestly, I couldn't blame them. New Era offered them a way out of poverty even if it was for only six months. Zane came back a few minutes later and surprisingly asked to brainstorm with me. Hopefully, he's being sincere.

In the midst of our strategy planning, I interrupted and said, "The woman I'm meeting tonight name is Amanda. Do you know her?"

"Haha. She's the fattest one and gets tired pretty quickly. I don't think you should have any problems pleasing her. She likes to rant about her husband during intercourse. It's really weird, bro."

"Sounds like Katherine all over again." We laughed so hard that Zane almost fell out of the chair.

"Was it that bad, bro?"

"You just don't know."

Over the next hour, Zane and I strategized. Then, he

said he was going out to bring some guys to hear us. I changed clothes and waited.

———

The office staff left for the day and Jafari showed up a few minutes late with two other guys. When they came, you can see the group that was there weren't taking us serious; often giggling and playing on their phones.

"So, why are we here?" One of them yelled.

"Well, if this is all of you here, I'm going to begin."

"This agency has been in some deep shit lately and I'm warning you. Be careful from now on." I looked around, making eye contact with all of them.

"Careful? Careful of what?" One laughed sounding like a horse, causing the rest erupt. I knew this would happen.

"Okay, let's get cut the bullshit. New Era will began selling many of you, amateur models in the next few week. You're conceded as their property and before it's too late, I wanted to let you know."

The room suddenly went silent, realising I wasn't messing around.

"What do you mean?" One man said terrified.

"Exactly as you heard. You will be sold meaning cheaper wages and paying your own rent. It's time to figure out what to do next. My advice is to that you do your best to impress or else."

The guys were confused but optimistic. During the

next hour, they sat and we tried answering questions. Most of them I couldn't answer or wouldn't because of what I heard from Benjamin.

It felt like we were starting an uprising but was it a smart idea? I'm risking my life and livelihood to save others. What I didn't tell them was about the escort services and it probably was wise not to.

"Hopefully it works out for all of us. I have to leave you guys now." I said putting on my jacket.

"Thanks, man."

"No problem." With that, I hurried downstairs, cutting it close to my appointment with Amanda. I had the address of the Mandarin Oriental hotel written down and was prepared to meet my doom.

———

Who is Amanda? I pondered while sitting in the taxi. What can I do to get out of this? Nothing. Once I got to the hotel, the front entrance was guarded by two doormen and two armed guards. Ines wasn't lying when she said it was five stars.

The guards inspected my New Era ID and then permitted me to head to reception. There was a petite brunette standing at the desk, smiling.

"Bonsoir, sir. Do you have a reservation?" she kindly asked.

I nodded. "Oui, for Room 107." I crossed my arms

waiting. She looked on the computer screen for the next minute.

"No need for keys tonight, sir. Your host's already waiting for you inside. The suite is straight ahead on the ground floor. Have a lovely stay."

"Merci."

My hands got sweaty, and I became nervous as I approached the room. This felt weirder maybe because Zane already described her.

I knocked on the door and stepped aside. Seconds later, it opened, revealing Amanda. Her hair was dark, reaching her shoulders while her weight would be an issue. She wore mascara and had wrinkles on her neck. *What did I get myself into?*

I grinned slightly, and she smiled back but turned away bashfully. "A shy Madame? That's a first." I thought to myself.

"Come in. You're Abbasi, right?"

"Oui, and you're Amanda, I see. It's nice to meet you."

She offered her hand, which I gently kissed and handed me a check before we started. I will be a gentleman for this occasion, unlike when I was with Katherine. Amanda seemed different, but she's still a snake.

"Would you like something to drink?" she offered while holding up a glass which resembled scotch.

"I'm good, thank you." There was an uncomfortable feeling in the room. Her presence was awkward. I knew I had to make the first move though. Zane mentioned she was tired out easily, so I wouldn't have a problem pleasing her. I leaned in and kissed her gently. It was to her liking since she cupped my face and came closer. Her mouth was warm, and the caress of her lips was softer than I imagined.

She didn't stop. It turned into a make-out session quickly, which was tons of heavy lifting. I put her head downwards and she kept sucking my cock; gasping for air. Now, I was on top of her; moving her stomach out the way and sucking her big breasts. Her hair kept getting in the way which was nerve-wrecking. Then, I went down to her clit and lick it sensually; causing her to moan loudly. *Everybody probably heard us now!* I felt her heart pounding and it made me grin. I pulled her closer and sank my cock into her vagina, causing her to be a mess of never-ending yelling. I knew she was already out of it. After five minutes, she was creaming on my cock and said she was tired.

Amanda stretched out on the bed, with a wide smile on her face; enjoying it the moment. I didn't break a sweat, so I started pacing around the room with a glass of scotch in my hand, listening to her talk about her husband, of course. After five minutes, Amanda was sound asleep. She was a gentle giant for someone who was so crooked.

I didn't know if I should've leave her on the bed by herself. I didn't want to stay, so I wrote her a note saying I had a wonderful time with her and was looking forward to meeting her again. I knew she would swoon over me. This woman is almost the same age as my mother, but doing these immature acts.

Leaving out, I gave the receptionist a small tip. Once outside, the cold air of the night smacked me in the face. I needed it to so I could clear my head. I decided to take a walk and watched dozens of couples holding hands and looking happier than ever. All were enjoying their lives together without a worry in mind. Meanwhile, I wondered what life would be like here if I wasn't a *boy toy in Paris?*

6

À BON CHAT, BON RAT

TWO CAN PLAY THAT GAME

Two weeks had passed since we told the group about New Era and since first meeting Amanda. Since then, we had three hookups. Afterwards, she'd lie on my chest and talk until she fell asleep. Jafari got in touch with Sarah and started hooking up with her again. She was impressed by his looks, so she said that she would help him land an exclusive pinup in her upcoming edition and future gigs. Once his contract's over with New Era, he had guaranteed work with Sarah as long as he doesn't mess up.

Benjamin texted me earlier in the day to meet him at Ten Belles, a coffee shop near the centre of Paris. It's been a few weeks since we last met although we texted each other a few times here and there. Benjamin entered Ten Belles, looking groomed for once and walked right over to my table. "Sorry I'm late buddy, fucking traffic is a nightmare coming in-town."

"It's fine. I just got here about ten minutes ago."

"Abbasi, I recently was cleaning my apartment out - *don't laugh* - and while I was moving stuff around, I found something that can help us." I rubbed my eyes, excited at the news. Benjamin then reached in his pocket and pulled out a flash drive.

"What do you have there?"

"A while ago, while I was at New Era, I recorded a bunch of conversations between Pauline and myself. Unfortunately, almost all of them got spoiled. Anyway, I used to work in her office as a secretary. One evening, I was working late when a woman named Lilith came by. I believe that she was part of the original five group of sponsors, but don't hold me to that. Anyway, she left long before you got to the agency. In this recording, she keeps sobbing about not wanting to be a part of something. Unfortunately, things didn't go well in the end. Listen to it when no one is around. No need to tell anyone about this yet. Don't lose the flash drive or get caught with it."

"Of course, I won't." I replied.

"Yeah, Benjamin, I forgot to mention New Era will start selling our contracts to others. They're in a financial crisis."

His eyes widened and he looked disgusted.

"They will begin forcing the lowest from amongst us to accept their terms or else. I spoke to a selected group to get the word out."

"That's horrible. We need to hurry up."

"By the way, I've been given to a new woman named

Amanda. This Madame's getting too attached. I don't know what to do."

He waved his hand. The waiter came up, serving us our cups of coffee. "I remember her. Be careful and watch out for her husband. If he finds out she's having another affair, he will go nuts. The funny thing is that he never will divorce her. That guy's a fucking weirdo." *What kind of a husband wouldn't leave such a relationship?*

"What I also remember about her is that she lives alone now. After the first few affairs, her husband got fed up and left with their kids."

He went on to say: "We can coerce her in being a witness whenever we're ready to take our case to Interpol, otherwise no one will believe us."

My eyes popped. "Wait, we're taking this to Interpol? I didn't know we were going to be getting this deeply involved." Pauline was clever and could turn this against all of us like she did with Benjamin's career.

"What do you expect for God's sake? We're talking about fucking prostitution and human trafficking here. This isn't a case to go to *la police*."

"I might be a witness when the evidence mounts up. Don't count me out. For now, what we need you to do is to get to the money sources of New Era; the five hags if you know what i mean?"

"I agree but I have no relationship with Pauline. Only Ines, the damn snake. Remember, I tried breaking in Pauline's office a couple of weeks ago, but I couldn't get inside her computer."

Benjamin paused for a second, looking up at the ceiling as if he was thinking hard about something. Then, he resumed.

"I think Pauline daughter's birthday is this month. She used to brag about it all year long. She's so obsessed with her daughter. That rich spoiled brat. From what I remember, New Era celebrates every birthday with a huge party."

"Keep on talking, Ben. By night's end, we could have New Era closed in a matter of days."

"Haha."

"Try to remember when if you can?" I said taking out my phone to enter it.

After a minute, Benjamin said, "230898.

"Oh, my God! Ben, that might be the code to her computer as well as the cabinets."

It was clear he wanted payback for losing his reputation. Benjamin and I chatted for a bit longer. He was sure our plan would work if I could dig up dirt on the rest of the women.

I got back home, thinking about the woman Ben mentioned; Lilith James. *Did she leave New Era on her own or was she forced out? Was she one of the original sponsors of New Era?* Ben texted me more information on Lilith as the night went on. Lilith's reputation was tainted like Benjamin's and she decided to stay away out of the public's eye. During her tenure at New Era, the business flourished.

"Where were you?" Jafari said when he saw me come inside the cafeteria.

"I went to meet Benjamin Rinaldi. We have some more information." I smiled as he clasped his hands together in joy.

"What do you?"

"I can't say for now but I will tell you about it when it's time."

As I ate, Jafari kept gushing on about Sarah. He went to her house earlier in the day. I think the boy's pussy-whipped.

"I wish I could afford a place like hers one day. Man, she's so different. I've never met anyone like her."

I busted out in laughter. "You're catching feelings now, bro. Huh? Damn, she got you like that." *At least, Jafari's mind was occupied with something other than Pauline and Ines's wickedness.*

The cafeteria got crowded and a group of boys came up to me, shaking hands. I didn't need all that attention, so I told Jafari I was going upstairs.

"See ya, man."

Jafari stayed downstairs while Zane was out for the day with his Madame. A perfect opportunity to listen to the recording. *A few moments of privacy in this place was nearly impossible.*

I grabbed my laptop from under the bed and popped in the flash; which contained one folder reading AAA00321. I sure hope it's not a virus. I sat back, and

after ten seconds in, a female voice sobbing, most likely
Lilith's:

> *"It wasn't my fault. It was raining and I couldn't see where I
> was going. He was drunk and he kept on grabbing me by my
> hair, trying to pull me closer. He was trying to put my head
> down his privates. The moment my eyes were off the road, from
> the corner of my eye, I could see blinding lights, and something
> was coming from the other lane."*

"What's she talking about?" I first thought after
pausing it. It was Lilith, the woman Benjamin had
mentioned. It sounds like she was involved in a car accident. But why was this relevant? I continued listening.

> *"The dark road had a lot of curves. He kept grabbing the
> wheel, forcing me to do what he asked. I lost control of the
> steering wheel and we ended up driving into a ditch."*

Her sobs overtook the recording, but then another
person began speaking, Pauline:

> *"I know it was his fault, but you will have to compensate us on
> the price of my loss, my dear Lilith. Thirty grand and no one
> will ever know about this."*

Pauline is so God damn insensitive. She's a fucking
monster.

"What? I can't do that, Pauline. That man's family needs to know. I will be the one bearing the consequences for the rest of my life."

In between sobs, Pauline told her to calm down and she would take care of everything. The recording then ended.

"Fuck." *This can't be, I wanted to know more. What happened to her after this?* There were still many unanswered questions and I can't ask the devil herself.

Where's Lilith staying? I have to find her. Suddenly, Zane busted through the door, pouting. I shut my laptop quickly. Something's wrong.

"What is it?" Zane's body language was awful. It had to be bad.

"It's my boy, Dimitri. Ines told him to get ready to transfer by tomorrow morning. It's exactly what you said."

"Dimitri. Where's he now?" I jumped out of the bed, lacing up my sneakers.

"He's in his room. Man, he's freaking out, Abbasi. It's serious. The boy might kill himself." I stormed out the room and followed Zane's lead to Dimitri's room.

He was sitting on his bed with a knife in his hands, bloody while his two roommates were trying to calm him down.

"What's going on, Dee?" He looked on the verge of giving up on life and his eyes were red as Mars.

"They are going to sell me, Abbasi. Please help or I will kill myself tonight."

"Okay, calm down, and give me the knife. I got a plan. At 3 A.M., sharp, meet me down in the kitchen. I'll get you out. Pack only what you need and don't be late." Zane looked at me confused by what I said.

"Can I talk to you for a second, bro?"

"You're not serious. Are you? They'll find him the moment he leaves and it'll be the end for him. He belongs in a mental hospital for God's sake. Look at him."

"Do I have a choice? What should I do, leave him here to die or help him escape?"

Zane looked at me frustrated. *Shit, I know the feeling.*

"I'll make something up whenever New Era finds out. Don't worry."

I looked back at Dimitri, who was watching us. I smiled, leaving Zane to help clean the guy up. Dimitri's roommates helped him calm down and pack his things. I whispered to Dmitri once he left, go straight to the Russian consulate.

I went back upstairs and told Jafari what had transpired. He offered to help, but I told him I had things under control.

"I'll cover you just in case someone notices you left. Don't worry, it won't be like last time."

"You better." I replied.

———

The hours into the evening went by quickly and it was almost 3 a.m. I grabbed my phone and tiptoed out of the room. Jafari tried to stay awake but fell asleep on the living room couch. The suspense of the situation kept me awake for the entire night.

The hallway lights were dimmed and I heard the boys' snoring as I passed by their rooms. The elevator was shut off after 12, so I would have to take the stairs.

The lobby was dark and I didn't see the guard on duty which was unusual. I went to the kitchen and stood behind the door. "Where the fuck is Dimitri?" I thought. I waited and waited thinking he might've had a change of heart when a tall shadow slowly was approaching the direction of the kitchen. He was dressed in all black, carrying a big knapsack.

"You're ready?" He nodded looking drowsy. The fire exit in the kitchen was always kept unlocked. Most of the boys used it to sneak girls in and out at night and pay the guard to keep quiet. I only hope Dimitri will be safe once we leave.

The streets around New Era had very little lighting, and no one was walking around. Dimitri wasn't in the mood for talking as his mind was occupied on what could happen next. Zane booked a room at a nearby hotel and later before noon, he planned to go to the Russian consulate to seek help.

"Thank you for helping me. I appreciate it, man."

"Don't mention it. I had to. I'm so sorry I tried to get you in Ines's private lessons. I didn't know."

"Thank God."

We made it to the hotel after fifteen minutes of walking and was relieved that they were open 24 hours. Dimitri went to the reception and took the room keys. The desk clerk resembled a model in the latest Vogue magazine.

"Merci Beaucoup, Abbasi" Dimitri said as I shook his hand.

I gave him my cell number to call when he was home safe and headed back to New Era.

The kitchen's fire exit was still open. *Thank God!* Jafari was still sleep on the couch while Zane was out with a Madame. I drifted off to sleep, reflecting on Dimitri and his journey.

———

Jafari awakened me a few hours later. He was pulling on the edge of my bed, repeating my name. "What, what, what?" I responded, rubbing my eyes.

"Ines told everyone down to the hall now. Hurry up." Sounds like New Era just found out about Dimitri. Jafari waited for me as I got dressed.

Everyone was in the lobby puzzled on why she called us downstairs so early. Francois and Pauline were standing next to her and were whispering to each another. The guys were looking at me as if I had done something wrong.

It was obvious they found out about Dimitri running away. *"Are they mad because I helped him?"*

My eyes centered in on Ines. She looked towards everyone while we expected her to yell.

"You may or may not have known, one of your colleagues has gone missing from New Era early this morning. Our CCTV captured two boys running out from the fire exit in the kitchen late last night. Whoever accompanied Dimitri, please step forward."

Everyone's eyes turned towards me. I knew I had to do to take the blame. If I didn't, then our plan would be foiled. I took a deep breath.

"It was me." I said stepping forward. "I helped him leave. He was going to kill himself." There were sighs from Francois and Pauline.

"No surprise to me that it was you, Mr. Abbasi." Ines commented without emotion. Pauline was visibly upset and left.

"Come with me, Mr. Abbasi," she ordered. I pushed my way through the crowd of boys.

I looked like I was a criminal. Francois ordered everyone to go back to their rooms while I followed Ines to her office. She didn't say a word until I closed her door.

"Where is he?" She hit her desk forcefully.

"Answer me, now" she warned. *Dimitri probably was on a flight back to Moscow by now.* I laughed. Her face turned red and she was fuming.

"Do you feel betrayed?" I laughed and couldn't believe I was saying this to her face.

"Answer my fucking question, Abbasi," she pressed on. I didn't give in, but keep staring.

"I have nothing to say." I aggravated her more.

"You will pay dearly, Abbasi. Don't make me fire you and leave you to live in the streets of Paris. Remember your passport's with us, locked away. Or maybe you would like to start working for free?" Her words shocked me and her voice was eery.

"Ok. Ok. Let me tell you what happened to Dimitri. His father suffered a heart attack yesterday evening and he had to leave right away."

She paused, dissecting my words. "And if that's true, why didn't he tell me first?"

"It was late and he was scared to say anything. He didn't want to be embarrassed by the boys. It happened suddenly. You know Dimitri is very attached to his family." *Damn, I'm a good liar.*

"I don't know Abbasi, I don't know if I can trust you." She peeped her eyes at me, making me look away.

"I have no reason to lie to you. It doesn't concern me, really." I sombered as if I was telling the truth.

She kept silent for a while, but then spoke, "Give me his number. The one I've been calling is out of service."

"I don't have another number either. If you can't reach him and neither can I." *Lying to Ines felt so stimulating.*

"You're dismissed."

Dimitri had a good heart. I remember him telling me about his life back in Russia, and how he was so happy about getting this job. Turns out it was for the worst.

"Maybe you can call the Russian embassy and see if they know how to contact him?" I said leaving out of her office.

As I went back downstairs, I made prayers for Dimitri. I would try to call him later but I doubt he'd pick up. If he gets back home, the rest of us could as well. I just hope the Russians don't send him back here.

———

Nobody was in the room. Maybe the boys were out shopping or something. I need this time to block everything out. But damn, I need to get Lilith's information. Time is moving fast. Every day, we are at risk of being sold. This is so heartbreaking.

"Did you find out anything about Dimitri?" It was Jafari said when he got back.

I shook my head. "No, I'll try to call him later. I hope he made it to the consulate."

"What did you say to Ines?"

"Nothing really. Bro, I can't control myself around her. She irks the shit out of me"

We erupted in laughter.

"Do you have any plans when this is all over?"

Jafari's question made me think. I only knew about Cameroon, nothing else. Another modelling job here would be good though if the circumstances were right. If we exposed New Era, everyone would know about it and it may tarnish our modelling careers forever regardless. Maybe I can help Dad start a new business with the money I saved. I haven't spent much since I arrived.

"I'll probably go back home and help Dad start a business."

Jafari seemed confused. He has a job waiting for him with Sarah if he acts right. His salary might double from what this hell hole is paying us. I am happy for him and he deserves it.

After our chat, I called Benjamin. He must give me more on Lilith.

"Hello?" After two rings, he answered. His voice sounded groggy, probably because I woke him.

"Hey, sorry to disturb. But can you tell me where Lilith stays?"

"Hold on. Let me see if I can find out." He put me on hold for almost five minutes and then said, "84 Square de la Couronne. Pray she answers the door."

"Thanks and sorry for disturbing...."

"Wait, bud, I forgot to tell you. I might have some information on the escort she was with that night. He might not be dead after all. Don't say anything until I know for sure."

"What? Who is he? When?"

"Just keep your mouth shut about it until I have more details."

With that, he hung up, leaving me mystified. We were playing with fire and Pauline was the dragon.

———

New Era has a big photoshoot later today for L'Officiel. Two of our models got selected to pose and Ines required everyone who didn't have work to attend. Fortunately, I had a doctor's appointment, so it was the perfect excuse to miss out. I left out early to avoid making a scene.

"Where to?" the taxi driver asked. His car reeked of cigarettes. I grabbed my nose and handed him the address. He saluted and started the engine. It was a long ride, and we entered the countryside outside of the capital. I was worried about the bill, and the driver grinned as I kept on peeking at the meter. Suddenly, he turned it off.

"Thank you," I remarked. *You don't find many nice taxi drivers here.*

The scenery on the way was breath-taking. I took pictures marvelling at its surrounding. We passed a bunch of huge mansions until we came to a street, no cars could pass through. There were too many holes. I paid the driver and examined the long road noticing an old mansion at the end. Walking ahead, I would never guess somebody lived there. In skepticism, I wavered whether I was at the right place. Once I came to the doors, I opened the gates which made a big screech causing me cringe.

I knocked lightly on the tall black door, remembering Benjamin's words. She didn't answer, but I stood patiently. A few more knocks and I heard footsteps coming. It had to be her. "Hello? Lilith, It's Abbasi, a model at New Era. I need to talk to you about something urgently. Can you please open the door?" I pleaded as there wasn't no immediate reply.

Suddenly, the door cracked, and came out a middle-aged woman with a puzzled face. "Who are you again?" she spoke holding the door with all her might.

"I'm a model at New Era. My name is Abbasi." Once she heard "New Era", she gasped and shut the door. I waited and then knocked again.

"Please, I need you to answer some questions about that evil place." I wouldn't leave until she hears what I have to say.

"Also, I have a recording of possibly you on it." I yelled without thinking. Benjamin told me to keep it hush, but I didn't listen. The door unlocked again, and she stepped aside, inviting me inside.

"Come in, please."

There was a long hall with oak doors aligned on each side perfectly. This woman appears to have good taste.

"It has been a while since I heard anything about that agency." She led the way to her living room. It wasn't too fancy and had a historic look. I wasn't sure how to start off the conversation, without antagonizing her.

"I listened to a recording involving you and Pauline about a car accident. I need to ask you about Pauline and

New Era." She pointed to a couch gesturing me to sit. Then, she offered me a glass of wine. "Are you one of her escorts or pets?"

"No to pets and sadly, yes to being an escort." *I wonder how she knows?*

"Pauline is the devil herself and Ines and Francois are just her little puppets."

"Why are you here exactly? Questions aside." She took a seat staring directly at me.

I felt uneasy by her question. "I came to see if you could help me end this foolishness for good."

She chuckled. "Stop it? I mean there's no ending it. Pauline's the master of disguise and has everyone fooled including the damn mayor himself. I've tried and paid heavily for doing so." She took a long sip and set her glass on the table.

"I'm not going to give up easily." I said making myself clear. I know that the public didn't hear about the tragedy because Pauline had her people bury the story. I also heard that your family found out somehow and now you're estranged from them. A friend named Benjamin Rinaldi told me what happened."

"Oh, you know Benjamin. Good ole' Ben was a fighter but like me didn't succeed. Honestly, I believe that you're wasting your time here, my friend. There isn't anything we can do." She said pulling out a cigarette to light up.

"Maybe or maybe not. Anyway, how did you first

become part of New Era?" I sense she still felt intimidated by Pauline.

She hesitated to speak, giving my question some thought.

"I need to know this in order to help me and my friends from becoming trafficked." I pleaded.

Then, she broke her long silence. "Back when Pauline founded New Era, she was broke. Didn't have a single cent, so she made a contract with me and the rest of the four women. We were the well-known millionaire wives club of Paris. Our goal was to build our brand to expand globally. Pauline promised to connect us with those agencies in the America. We gave her a vote of confidence and promised to support. The rest of the wives wanted other favours as well. Pauline came up with the idea of using some models as sex slaves and the the group agreed except for me."

Her statement shocked me.

"Are the rest still part of the group?"

"Every single one. Since, New Era's brand has become global, and Pauline did what ever we asked her to do."

"Do you all own the same business chains?" I asked curious to know.

"We don't do the same thing. Katherine and her husband have a jewellery company. Amanda's an owner of a bank, and her husband's an interior designer. Marie has a chain of restaurants all over Paris. They are all very popular. Amy inherited her wealth from her father.

He was a loan shark and her family has small businesses all over France. The last one is Leonarda. I must admit she's the scariest, has done a lot of illegal things here in France. She's the wife of a politician in Paris. He hides her dirty work and they're all one happy family."

I was shocked about how much she knew. I had the urge to ask her more but I wanted to offer something. *Would she agree?*

"Let's end this now, Lilith. Let's report these gangsters to the Interpol." She looked at me as she sipped her drink.

"It's either the women or New Era."

"What do you mean?" I said puzzled by her response.

"Pauline is way smarter than you think. She's built a fortress. Just in case someone gets caught, she has a contract on them. The millionaire wives were required to sign contracts with her as well."

I couldn't believe I was duped into this.

"We can get to them. There has to be a way. They're destroying our lives as well as yours. Why not make them pay for they've done?"

She paused, licking her lips. "I like your bravery, Abbasi. I hope we can bring them down."

"We will."

We shared a few drinks as she told me stories about her life and family. I did the same. My courage impressed her, and she told me she'd never intended on doing anything illegal with the models. This was the main reason she quit New Era.

There was work ahead for us to get the women to confess especially those who I haven't been with yet. I believe I have Katherine and Amanda in the palm of my hands. Zane could help me get to the rest. Unfortunately, he wants to continue working as an escort deep down inside. All thoughts and more running through my mind as I made it to my doctor's appointment on time and headed back to New Era.

"He Zane,, can I talk to you for a minute?" Zane was in the lounge room, playing games. He lowered his headphones and looked up.

"What's up, bro?"

"I need you to tell me about Marie, Leonarda and Amy."

"What you want to know?" I could sense others around him listening in, so I pointed towards the hall. He followed me and when we were alone, he said what do you want to know?

"You gave them some love, right?"

He yawned. "Yeah, why do you ask?" "Nothing special except that I need to know what they're like because I may ask Ines to hook a boy up. It can't be that hard?" I giggled, and he finally put down his guard.

"What happened Abbasi? Are you quitting this revolution of yours?"

I nodded. "I guess so. I need to make some more

money. Someone in my family is sick. Now, Ines has this place on lockdown."

He patted my back as if I was joining the dark side. He must be mistaken.

"Let me start with Amy. She's a sweetheart but feisty and always wants to be on top. She isn't married anymore and is back living with her parents. They're so old they probably believe that you're their child when they meet you."

"Haha. You're funny."

I was stunned, wasn't she forty years old? That's weird.

"Give her roses every time you meet and you'll get a huge tip."

"What about Marie?" Looking around, I made sure nobody was eavesdropping.

"She's had a lot of affairs with men. Her beauty has everyone mesmerised. She got some good men in trouble."

"Is she married?"

"Yeah. Her husband is thirty years older than her though. It's creepy. They don't even sleep in the same room."

"Let me tell you about Leonarda."

"Ok."

"You need to be mindful of her. She will never let you come alone to her place and always likes to meet at five-star hotels. She likes gangbangs. Literally, she runs the guys around like she's acting in a damn movie. She tells the males that she's their goddess. One time, she gave us ten thousand euros to split, all because one guy in a costume put on an act for her."

"Get the fuck out of here, man. Is her pussy made of gold or what? This is outrageous."

"I'm serious, bro. She's very picky about everything."

This will be a big dilemma. I know Ines wouldn't put me with her but somehow I'll find a way.

7

J'EN METTRAIS MA MAIN AU FEU!

"I'D PUT MY HAND IN THE FIRE!"

Lilith and I came up with a strategy on how to catch the millionaire wives. The plan was to ask Ines to pair me with them, the one thing we both would agree to only if I gave up my salary. Lilith kept in touch with the women and knew exactly what each of them liked. She'd pick me up, bring me to the meeting locations and then hide while recording our conversations. We'd then used the recordings to blackmail the women in becoming witnesses. Sounds like a plan!

I wanted to say something to Jafari, but Lilith told me to keep this between us. It was best to protect everybody. Our first target would be Katherine. I told Ines I wanted to meet her again to make up for what happened and that I'd forfeit my pay and tips in exchange. Surprisingly, she accepted and planned for us to meet at a hotel downtown.

Lilith arrived, waiting outside the hotel in her car

while I got there a bit earlier, hanging out in the lobby. Katherine was running late. She told Ines that she was thrilled about meeting with me again, but little did she know.

I walked up to the desk of the receptionist to inquire about the room. *"Ms. Katherine will be fifteen to twenty minutes late due of traffic."*

"Ok. I have a surprise for her. So, would you mind giving me the keys to our room?" I said excitedly. *"Surely, sir."* She gave them to me and I texted Lilith to come inside and meet at the elevators. Lilith hurried and we went up together. She checked the hallway to see if anyone was around while I opened the door.

"I'll be in the closet. You just entertain her until it's time for me to come out. I have this for the special occasion." Lilith pulled a gun from her back side, which made me jump back.

"Wow, what the hell are you doing? You never said anything about guns." What if something goes bad, we'd get caught. I couldn't even imagine how many years we would be in prison.

"Relax, Abbasi. It's not loaded. I'll just scare her a little bit. Who's knows maybe she'll piss in her pants?"

We chuckled. *Seriously, let me take a long deep breath.* I threw my backpack on the table and headed to the bathroom to freshen up.

"Ines's so dumb. This will be easy." I said before going inside.

Lilith giggled, shaking her head in agreement. "She

tries to play this role of a tough guy when she's the exact opposite."

Ten minutes later, there was a loud knock on the door. "Katherine. Quick, hide," I whispered as I made my hair and opened my robe looking sexy. Lilith hid in the closet, fastening her gun on her backside. Before I opened, I stood and made a quick prayer.

Swinging the door open, I looked at Katherine with a glare of fiery desire. Katherine was standing there seductively grinning in a black slip dress. "Long time, no see Abbasi." She embraced and grabbed my face. "Oui, Katherine, mon amour. Come in."

Grabbing me passionately, she already dragged me to the bed while the door was still open. "Ok, dear. Relax. Let's have a drink first." She giggled while I poured her a glass of wine from the room's bar and then I went to close the door. I need to buy some time. She drowned the glass and then hot damn, she pushed me down to jump on top of me, ready to fuck.

"Slow down, mon amour. We have time." Laying on the bed, half-naked, I almost fell asleep listening to her nonstop talking. I can only imagine Lilith telling me to speed things up. Then, when she was about to go on and speak, I met my lips onto hers, snatching her. She vigorously unbuttoned my pants and quickly removed her clothes.

She then began licking the head of my cock as I prayed Lilith would come in before we really started fucking. Then, my prayers were answered.

"Hello, Katherine. It's been a while."

Katherine froze at the dark voice. Then, frantically turned around, seeing Lilith standing above her.

In complete shock, Katherine almost forgot how to talk, mumbling and fumbling her words. "I, I, I…"

"Lilith, what the hell are you doing here?" She grabbed the bed sheets in hysteria, trying to cover herself as she looked confused.

"I'll do the questioning while you are here with us today." I jumped up out of the bed, pulling my pants up. Lilith had the gun pointed at her and had a mean look on her face.

"What is the hell is this?" Katherine raised her voice. "I'm not saying anything and you!" She said pointing at me. "You're in big trouble, Monsieur." Katherine stood up and looked as if she was heading to the door.

"For us not to tell your family and business partners about your secret love affairs with these boys, you do as I fucking say. Sit your ass down or else we'll have some cleaning up to do." Katherine's face was astonished at Lilith's words. She gave me goose bumps. Katherine was tough and I think she would beat the shit out of her if she had to.

"Come on and put on your damn clothes. We don't have all fucking day, Kathy." Lilith said waving the gun in front of her face. Getting dressed, she sat nervously on the bed while giving us looks of disgust.

"Okay, Katherine. Let's begin with recording number two."

"Number Two?" Katherine shouted.

"Yes, number two. I fucking said. Number one was the sex scene you were doing with Abbasi. Maybe you can audition for a part in the soft porn one day."

That made me laugh.

Lilith went on to say, "You'll listen and answer every single one of my questions and admit to your wrongdoings or else you will die today." She scowled and didn't waste any time on starting the device.

"What is your business with New Era modelling agency?"

I already knew everything. Katherine took a long deep breath, shaking her head, looking as if she was about to cry.

"Answer the damn question." Lilith looked devilish.

"I entered into a contract with them about two years ago, for business purposes as access to the models."

"What kind of fucking access?" Lilith shouted.

"They were given to me to enjoy." And just like that she began sobbing.

"Did the models agree to these terms?" Lilith pressed on.

"No. I don't think so." Katherine cried out.

"How many models were your sex slaves in the last two years?" Lilith kept pressing. I could feel the bitterness in her words. It was horrifying, too intense for me, so I looked away.

"There were nine, in total. I'm very sorry." She said trying not to cry but failed. She broke down into long-winded sobs. Lilith signalled that her interrogation was done and stopped the recording device. Then she packed up while not saying a word.

"What will you do with that tape, Lilith? What do you want from me? I'll give you anything."

"I don't want anything from you, Katherine. If you're not stupid enough to tell anyone about this, it will stay locked away, perhaps forever. If you are, the entire world will know about the devilish things you've done. Oh, don't bother asking for Abbasi for your evil fetishes or any of the models ever again." Lilith looked at her like the devil himself. Just like that we were out the door.

We had just ended the career of one of the monsters in this criminal enterprise. Katherine was left speechless. She'd most likely would keep quiet, but I knew Lilith wouldn't uphold her end of the bargain.

"What are we going to do with the tapes?" I asked as we were leaving the hotel. "I'll email them to the Interpol when the time comes. We must get all five women to confess, otherwise it will be easy for them to deny it. You didn't buy the whole-keeping-them-locked-up thing, did you?"

Her quirky face made me smile. It felt good being winners for once. I stopped outside to reflect on the hotel's grand stature. Lilith came on my path when I needed her the most and I would forever thank God for that. Drowned in thoughts, I didn't notice she was walking ahead of me. When I caught up, she said, "Let's go get some coffee and celebrate." This lady reminds me of my mother when she was younger.

————

The coffee shop wasn't packed but instead of sitting down inside, we went and sat on a bench at a nearby park. It's been a while since I felt this safe. It was strange being next to this woman who I only met close to a week ago. Perhaps she considers me as a son since she didn't have any contact with her children after the allegations. It's sad but maybe I'll be around when everyone learns about the truth. I had a feeling Lilith lived for that day, as sad as it sounded.

"The weather is nice today." she observed.

"It feels nice being away from New Era. I feel like a rebel leader there."

"You are."

She was right. My thoughts shifted to why did I not take the gun away from Lilith. I gave her the freedom to do the interrogation alone. Will I ever do the dirty work? Maybe, it's just not in me. "It was impressive what you did. I couldn't even think about doing something like that. I never held a gun in my life."

"When you lose so much, your emotions just suddenly turn off. You don't feel anything. For years, I've felt empty inside. I always thought this is the life I'll be living from now on. Might as well get used to it and live for the moment, you know."

I listened closely as her pain was visibly expressed. It made me think about the way I treat my parents.

"What about your family, where are they now?" She said while sipping.

I took a deep sigh. "My family's back home in Cameroon. They allowed me to come here, believing this was our way out of poverty and I'd make their lives easier. Little do they know how hard it is to do right here."

"I'm sure they appreciate what you are doing, and once they find out about your courage, believe me, they will be proud of you." Her words were comforting. I didn't want to see Mom's soul crushed because of my situation. The only thing I ever wanted was her happiness and home-cooked meals.

"Do you have any siblings?"

"I do. A younger sister that just started university."

"You need to do what you can for her."

In the middle of our conversation, we got interrupted by my phone ringing. It was Jafari. I answered, groaning, "Yes?" snapping at him. This guy never leaves me in peace.

"You need to come back to New Era. Ines's going around checking everyone's rooms for curfew. You know we have a curfew now because of Dimitri."

"Crap. I'm on my way." I cut the call. Lilith was puzzled.

"I need to leave right away."

"Ok. I'll give you a ride. It sounds urgent. Is everything okay?"

"Yes, just Ines checking our rooms to see if we're in for curfew."

"Yikes, I don't remember her being that strict."

"One guy named Dimitri ran away from New Era and now the place's on lockdown."

"I hope he made it out safely."

"I hope so, too."

———

Lilith sped down the highway and I prayed on the way I'd make it back in time. I could feel Ines' breathing down my neck.

I said goodbye to Lilith and promised to call when it was Amanda's time. I had to think of a lie to tell to Ines just in case. Aggravated by the thought, I used the staircase to get to the room and hoped for the best. Jafari unlocked the door finally after a few loud knocks.

"What took you so long?" I snapped, walking over to my bed and pulling the comforter over my body.

"I thought it was Ines. She already knocked twice. I acted as if I was asleep." *That was smart of him.*

"Where were you anyway?"

"Not now." I thought to myself.

"I'll tell you everything later." I said as I messed up my hair to look like I was sleeping.

"Fine." He replied as we waited for Ines to knock. We

didn't have to wait long. When after only a few minutes, she came banging on the door like a crazy woman.

"Open this door, now or I will call security!" Her voice was thundering as she kept banging with full force. I was surprised it didn't break it.

"Coming." I slurred, loud enough for her to hear. I opened the door seeing her look at me firmly. "May I help you?" I asked.

"I guess you didn't have time to change your clothes? You were supposed to be back from your meeting with Katherine two hours ago." She walked around our room while her eyes were fixed on Jafari. He pretended to be asleep, but I sensed he was trying his best not to laugh.

"I did, two hours ago, I was too tired to change, so I fell right asleep. Anyway, that's none of your business. I've done what you've asked of me." She knew her threats to me meant nothing. Ines didn't say a word afterward and left the room, slamming the door. Jafari and I let out sighs of relief.

"She's such a nuisance, bro. Damn, you got some balls boy talking to her like that." Jafari said.

"She knows what I do for her."

———

Three days later, after Ines had calmed down, she had surprisingly arranged for me to meet with Amanda. This time, I agreed to give her my pay but I'll keep the tips. I told her that I wanted New Era to remain open and I was willing to do this to help the company out. Maybe it will impress Pauline to get me to Leonarda.

The morning before meeting Amanda, I woke up late and was able to get some much needed rest. *Why's no one here? Was something scheduled today?* I jumped out of bed and got freshened up. Lilith would come pick me up a few blocks away in about ninety minutes.

I went downstairs for breakfast. Jafari and Zane were already eating. "I thought you would sleep all day." Jafari laughed. Zane didn't say anything.

"I forgot to set the alarm," From the corner of my eye, I saw Ines coming to the cafeteria. I looked her way. She kept peeping around until her eyes landed on me. "What's up with her today?" I said, my question directed towards Jafari.

"She's been acting weird since yesterday."

"So, did you get to meet the other women yet?" Zane asked.

"Only Katherine. I'm still working on getting with the others," He was more concerned about me fucking than what we needed to do. *How pathetic? He loves being a boy toy.*

"Am I missing out on something?" Jafari said with a mouthful of food.

"Not really, but I'll explain later."

He start pouting, "No, explain now. You told me that the other night when you came home late."

I chuckled and knew I had to say something. "I

agreed to see other women, you know, I need the money. My sister's in university now and her school fees are killing us."

Zane looked at me surprised while Jafari just shook his head.

"Oh, yeah right? My god, Abbasi that's really kind of you. What about shutting this shithole down?"

"It'll happen." I responded.

"I guess Playboy. This is disgusting. I'll see y'all later." Jafari's got up and stormed off, having a temper tantrum. I had to leave soon as well and Zane went about his business.

———

I phoned Amanda when I was outside the cafeteria. "Amanda, I'll be by in thirty minutes. Get ready and get sexy, mon amour." She texted me back saying, "Ok. How did you get my number?""

"You gave it to me after you creamed on me, remember? Now it's payback time."

"Umm, hmm. I did, didn't I? Ok, mon amour. Sure, but let's meet for coffee first."

I wasn't so sure if something was wrong. I texted her back saying, "Ok. Meet me at Bourlosque St. I'll be driving in town and will meet you outside the shop."

"Ok."

As soon as I got finished texting, I felt someone's lurking behind me.

"Don't go wandering around and don't be late. We need our clients pleased." It was Ines, hassling me as usual.

"I won't." I said giving her a fake smile and went about my business.

Walking out of New Era, I had a feeling that Ines sent some to spy on me. I texted Lilith. "Ines might send someone to follow me, so let's meet a few blocks away from our usual scheduled location." There were a back alleys that no one would go down except the homeless, so I cut through them to make my way to Lilith.

I ended up being late for our meeting. Lilith wasn't thrilled, and I explained to her my hunches. "I couldn't help it. I think Ines sent someone to follow me." Lilith looked back when she turned the ignition. *"No one's there."*

"I saw a security guard from New Era looking at me around the area of the Farmer's market. Maybe I'm just paranoid.

"Don't worry. Let's get out of here."

"Did you call contact Amanda?" she asked as we sped down the highway.

"Yeah, we'll meet her at Bourlosque St. I'll take over the wheel when we get there and you'll lay down under the covers in the back seat."

"Haha. Why not go to hotel this time?"

"Lilith said let's meet for coffee first." After a few minutes, we reached the place and switched places. Since Amanda hadn't arrive yet, we role-played the scene until she arrived. I texted Amanda where I was and after a few minutes, I saw her coming towards the vehicle. "She's coming." I whispered.

"What? Get ready?"

"Ok" I remained silent until Amanda got the door and she waved. I opened the door for her and she struggled to get in. I got out to help her and said, "Hey, Amanda. How have you been, mon amour?" I hugged her as if I haven't seen her for years.

I'm good. How are you doing?" She was acting suspicious. I remember Zane telling me she was very cautious.

"I'm yours for today. Let's go get some coffee."

"No, why don't we just drive around for a little while first?" *Interesting because that was the plan anyway.*

Lilith lingered underneath the blanket in the back and said nothing. Maybe she was waiting for the right moment? As I was driving around, I started the conversation. "So, what would like to do, besides circling Paris today, mon amour? I know we haven't been together for a while." It felt awkward just chatting.

"We can go anywhere you like, I don't mind." Then after a long pause, she asked, "Abbasi, by the way, how long have you been a model at New Era?"

"For only two months, why do you ask?" I was actually curious to know.

"I don't know. I just have an uneasy feeling. I don't want to keep doing this with you. I'm starting to feel bad about all this."

I stopped the car for a moment in traffic. *Would this mean she would stop seeing me and the rest of the boys?* I was somewhat happy, but wasn't sure whether Lilith would still proceed with the plan. We still needed her as a witness.

Pulling over to the side of the road, I replied "You know what, I'm actually glad you don't want to keep doing this. You seem like a nice lady. I don't know how you got caught up in this." My words didn't feel like any sympathies.

"I want to change my life honestly. If I can help you with anything, please tell me."

For a second, I thought she was faking or maybe she was on to us. It was weird.

"You can help him, by being a witness." Lilith finally rose from the back seat. Amanda screamed in fear and almost hit her head on the windshield. "Now, do you really want to stop doing this?" asked Lilith in the most demonic manner.

We gave her some time to gather herself and then she spoke. "What do you want me to say?" From the rear-view mirror, I saw Lilith unlocking her phone and pressing record.

"What is your business with the New Era modelling agency?"

"I am one of five women who sponsors New Era and uses their models as sex escorts." Amanda stated. I was happy she'd changed her mind.

"Did you force them?"

Amanda lowered her head, not being able to look at me. "They complied and followed my wishes, but I'm sure it was because they knew they would get in trouble with Pauline if they didn't abide by my wishes"

She, then gave me a look of pity; I turned away.

"Did you agree to conspire with New Era to cover this up and keep these sex services secret?" Lilith asked. Then, there was a long pause.

Amanda appeared to be in pain. "Yes, I did. I slept with over fifteen models. I'm so sorry. I want to change." she mumbled and then soon after began wailing. It was a memory I wouldn't forget.

"Thank you, Amanda, you've helped us so much with your testimony today." Lilith ended the recording.

She knew she'd have to face a lengthy prison sentence if this came out, but she didn't care. Amanda had regrets about doing this.

"I'm sorry for everything, Jafari. I hope you will forgive me someday." She smiled weakly at me.

"You're forgiven on one condition. Don't ever do this to any of us again."

"Yes, I promise with the life remaining in my soul, Abbasi."

My words made her smile and I cautiously unlocked the door of the car for her to get out.

Lilith and I went on staring at each other mischievously for a few seconds.

"I didn't think it would be that easy." she said.

I sighed. "Me neither."

She climbed back to the passenger seat and replayed the recording. We sat and talked in the car for a while, going over plans for our next targets. It wouldn't be as easy, since I never met Amy, Marie and Leonarda.

"I really don't know how we will do this." I said being honest. Lilith raised her eyebrows and shrugged. "It will be a piece of cake to get Amy and Marie to confess but Leonarda, she won't give in easily."

———

I'll began focusing my attention on Leonarda. Zane could help me but it would mean I'd have to tell him everything I know. Lilith drove me back to New Era and dropped me off at our usual spot. It was urgent for me to talk to Mr. Zane right away. We couldn't afford to lose time.

New Era hosted a week of outdoor photo shoots for two new fashion magazines interested in colloborating. Everyone was busy at the park, a block away from New Era, setting up decals while Trisha was busy inside organising the clothes inside with a few helpers. The gym was filled with racks of outfits, shoes and poster-boards. Zane was helping out or supposedly when I spotted him. As usual, he was with a group, horsing around.

"Hey, man. Can we talk for a minute?" I cut him off. The rest of the guys laughed for some reason. *Who knows why?* Zane acted like he was working out, climbing off the treadmill. "What is it now?"

I pulled him towards the corner. "How can I contact

Leonarda?" He looked at me as if I was crazy. The fact that I wanted the top dog bothered him.

"You can't. Only people with special permission and you're definitely not even close to getting it."

I wanted to smack the shit out of him. This guy's so annoying. "Well, do you know how I can get a chance to get in with her?" I demanded, not giving up.

"I don't but if you're lucky enough, maybe you can find a way to get invited to her upcoming birthday bash. It's a few days before Pauline daughter's." He smirked and then was about to leave when I grabbed his arm. "Birthday Bash? When is it?" He tried to pulling away but failed. "You won't get in, in a million years."

"Pauline and Ines will find out what you are up to. Since I heard you've been bad at pleasing these ladies, you'll be on Pauline's hit list if you don't man up."

"Where you got that from, bro? All the ladies I've been with have said nothing but daddy, daddy, daddy. Are you jealous?" Zane laughed at my comment and went back to his crew.

Pauline knew everything about me. I never talked to her but if she had a complaint, I would have heard it from Ines already. I guess it's time to go pay her a visit. Before so, Ines spotted me and asked me to give her a hand. *"Ugh!"*

———

Once I got finished with Ines, I didn't delay going to

Pauline's office. Let's see if Trisha is still there. *Oh snap! She looks like a new girl as a blonde.* She was sitting at her desk, painting her nails and looking beautiful as ever. Once she saw me, she cleared her throat and smiled.

"Is Pauline in?" I tried sounding serious.

"She's in a meeting at the moment. You can wait for her if you would like." She just kept smiling.

"Okay." I said sitting right next to her.

I saw her eyes on my cock and it made me feel uneasy. After doing her nails, she played with her hair, constantly looking at me as if I was her meal.

"So, what's new with you, Mr. Abbasi?"

"Nothing much. I'm here to ask Pauline to get some modelling advice." Trisha was nosy and always eavesdropped on everyone's conversations. No wonder why they call her Pauline's pet.

We sat in silence for a few minutes and it seemed to irritate her. *If only Pauline would come out right now?* I could see Trisha looking down at my cock as she did her work. I really wanted to give her something to think about with every second that passed. Finally, Pauline walked out the door in a rush and passed by Trisha. Trisha looked puzzled as she pointed in my direction.

"Abbasi, why are you here? I'm very busy."

"I need to speak with you urgently." I said while getting up from my seat. My cock was rock hard and Pauline raised her eyebrows; giving Trisha a stare before turning to me.

"Ok, let's talk in my office." She disappeared through

the door, leaving no choice but for me to follow her. I thought she would say something about my behaviour. Ines probably complained to her about me. I wasn't worried because I was one of her best models bringing her in big money.

"What did you want to talk about?" She said standing behind her desk, flicking on her computer. I scratched the back of my head and sat down.

"I'll get straight to the point."

"Go ahead."

"I want to take part in Leonarda's birthday bash. I know she only accepts the best and I feel I'd be a good fit. Plus, I need extra money as my sister and family are suffering back home due to the drought." *Man, I was getting good at lying.*

With a puzzled face, Pauline paused and then said, "I will add you to the list for next week. However, you need to be extra careful. Her family is politically connected. We don't want any troubles, Abbasi. Do you understand me?"

"Oui, Pauline. I understood completely." *That was easy.*

8

CHACUN VOIT MIDI À SA PORTE

"EVERYONE SEES NOON AT HIS OWN DOOR"

I researched that night finding what I could on the remaining three women starting with Amy who married three times. She's currently seeing a bodybuilder and have two young children. Her addiction was shopping as she was a regular at Le Bon Marché. Lilith and I paid her a visit one afternoon.

We were waiting right in front of the main entrance where she would go in regularly around 1 PM. Her personal driver was known to accompany her from time to time.

"Do you think this will be easy?" I said staring ahead at Amy. Lilith snickered, chewing on a burger she brought along.

"Yes. She is the dumbest out of all of them." We laughed and kept waiting. After two hours, there she was, her hands filled with so many bags along walking with her driver who looked overwhelmed. She dropped the bags to put her sunglasses on.

Before we could proceed, the driver opened the car door, loading the bags and Amy quickly got in. "Follow the car." Lilith ordered. I waited for them to pull off. "This driver's mad. Look at him speeding and switching lanes." I said. I wasn't sure if he knew we were following them.

They parked in front of Le Cinq (one of Paris's finest restaurants). Amy got out and was greeted by some other women; none of who we recognised. The driver drove off probably because she would be long.

Lilith began laughing. "Get ready to wait for another three hours."

I hope she isn't serious? "Isn't this too much?"

"Relax. You'll get out of the car and act as if her driver ordered for you to pick her up because of an acci-dent. That's why I rented this luxury sedan." Lilith started scrolling on her phone, without a single worry in mind. After almost 90 minutes, I began feeling hungry and tired. Looking around, I heard loud laughing coming from the front entrance. "Oh, it's Amy. She's coming out."

"Hey, it wasn't three hours after all."

"Lilith, get to the back seat now." I said straightening myself up. Looking presentable, I pulled up to the front entrance, and got out opening the door for her.

"Madame Amy, your driver sent me to pick you up. He was involved in an accident. Not serious but he would have been late, so he sent me." She widened her eyes in excitement.

"He did! Oh, that's such a relief. Que Dieu bénisse son âme."

I held the door for her, closing it and then got in.

Now, it was time for Lilith to step in. "Long time no see, Amy." I smirked the second Lilith spoke.

Amy jumped up and screamed. "Oh, mon Dieu!" Her voice was loud enough that people outside the car looked at us. I sped off just in time.

"Lilith, what are you doing here? What is this?" Although, I wanted to laugh, I couldn't take her seriously. The moment was pure comedy gold.

"You will answer a few questions or else we'll have a little problem. Won't we?" Lilith now had her gun out. The atmosphere became silent and I could only hear Amy whisper. "What do you want?"

"First, when did you sign the contract with New Era?"

"Why are you doing this? I don't want to go to jail."

"Answer me now or else." Lilith pressed the gun on her temple and I could hear Amy whimper.

"I don't know maybe close to two years. Please don't kill me." I started driving faster hoping nobody could see what was going on inside.

"Did you use the models in the agency for sex?"

From the corner of my eye, I saw Amy backing up to the windshield, afraid Lilith might kill her.

"Yes, but they enjoyed it. They were getting more money than New Era could ever offer them."

"How many have you slept with so far?"

"Only five of them" she answered shamelessly, as If it was something she could buy at the market. She might've been dumb but for sure she wasn't when she was with these young men.

"What if they didn't want to have sex for money?" Lilith repeated the sane question she asked Katherine and Amanda.

"Too bad. If they want to be models in this industry, they have to put in the time with us in bed." She had no remorse at all. I was disgusted and wanted her out of the car.

Lilith stopped the recording and turned to Amy, smiling. "Too bad, huh. Guess what! You will pay for Abbasi's time this afternoon. Send Pauline a message that you were pleased with him and make sure you add a tip or else. Also, if anyone finds out what we've discussed today, I'll send this damn tape to your father, ex-husbands, boyfriend and your kids in a heartbeat. If you keep your mouth shut, nothing will happen and it'll go all away. One more thing before I forget, make sure you never use these young men again for your little fetishes or else."

Amy quickly pulled out her checkbook, writing two checks;

TO: ABBASI ADEMOLI IN THE SUM OF TEN THOUSAND
EUROS.....
TO: NEW ERA IN THE SUM OF TEN THOUSAND
EUROS.....

I had to admit, Lilith looked scary and Amy looked like she was in a horror movie.

We took Amy at an unknown gas station and kept going.

"Only two left. I can't wait till this is over."

"You've been away from New Era too often for the past few days. I suggest you spend more time there. I'll be in touch."

Her sudden change confused me. Weren't we supposed to finish this as soon as possible?

"What's wrong?"

"Nothing. I just need some time to gather my thoughts. I want to call my family over to dinner since it's been a while. But I'm not sure if Richard will want to come. I miss my kids."

I could understand what she was feeling, and I felt at ease she told me what bothered her. It meant she trusted me and I was beyond grateful. "Call them over. I will explain everything to them." I had to do something for her in return. Even though my speech wouldn't cost a thing, I couldn't pay her back enough for what she had done for me.

"Wait, are you serious? You would do that?" Her eyes lit up, and her smile widened.

"For sure. Why not?"

She clasped her hands together in excitement. "I will call them over tonight. Make sure to get to my house extra early. I can't cook all by myself you know. I might mess up. It's been a while." We both agreed on cooking together and as always, she dropped me off at a nearby street of the agency.

I understand how she was feeling. Her telling me this meant she trusted me. "Call them over. I'll explain everything. Maybe they'll believe me." I had to do something in return for what she had done for me.

"Wait, are you serious? You would do that?" Her eyes lit up, and her smile broadened.

"For sure. Why not?"

She clutched her hands together in excitement. "I will call them over tonight. Get to my house extra early. I can't cook all by myself you know. I might mess things up. It's been a while." As always, she dropped me off at a few streets away from New Era.

I was in awe that I could help reunite a family. I wondered how her husband would react. I was sure I would get along just fine with her daughter since she was around my age. I couldn't fathom life without my parents, even at twenty years old.

———

Once I got back, Jafari was in the room raving about how much in love he was with Sarah. *This boy's crazy.*

"So, did she talk to her parents about you yet?" I dried my hair as I sat on the bed.

"No, I don't think so. If Ines gives me a day off, we can hopefully have dinner with them."

"Who gives a fuck about Ines? Have fun. It'll be for a few hours, nothing to worry about, man."

I was real with him as he was with me. Zane on the other hand, was fake as a mannequin. We couldn't have a regular conversation without him getting jealous.

Speaking of the Zane, he came in the room with a big grin on his face. I had the impulse to roll my eyes but I didn't. "Guess who just got to Leonarda?" Jafari was puzzled at Zane's sudden excitement. I knew what he was talking about.

"Who is Leonarda?" Jafari asked being nosy.

"She's the biggest of the five millionaire ladies, the specialist of BDSM. Jafari, you wouldn't know anything about that." He was talking as if he was above Jafari in some way.

"It's good that you're not part of it. You're not missing out on anything special. It's a lot of hardworking bullshit."

———

The hours were going by quickly. I started searching for recipes on the internet to make and came up with lasagna. I wasn't so sure if she would like it, so I wrote down a few others. Ines gave me a pass since Amanda paid extra, not knowing our encounter earlier in the day. On my way to Lilith's house, I went to the market and bought some stuff we needed. I would be bummed if she had already started cooking. Then again, I hoped they would eat everything.

I took a taxi and the fare was high since I stopped at the supermarket first.

Suddenly, I received a text message and guess who it was. It read:

Hey, Abbasi. This is Dimitri. I made it to Russia. The consulate got me out of the country. They had to print me a new passport since New Era held onto ours. My girlfriend and I are getting married soon. Also, I can testify via Skype if you need me. Let me know and take those fuckers down.

"Yes" I pumped my fist in the air as I knocked on the door of Lilith's house. She was a mess with flour covered all over her face.

"Are you okay?" I chuckled as I came in and handed her a bags of groceries.

"Yeah, I tried baking them a cake but probably messed it up." She took them to the kitchen and thanked me.

"What do you plan on cooking?" She yelled from the kitchen.

I took off my coat. "I was thinking maybe lasagna. I got everything to make it except I don't know how."

"Great idea. It's my daughter's favorite."

"So, they agreed to come over?" I made my way to the kitchen, seeing it was already a mess. It would be impossible to cook in there.

"It took a lot of convincing, but Richard gave in." She took the cake out of the oven.

"You don't cook often, do you?" I joked. The cake didn't look well baked.

"Does it look done?" She paused, looking straight at it.

"No, but I brought something else just in case." I walked over to where she left the groceries and pulled out a cake wrapped in a box. I opened it in front of her and she choked.

"You're a genius, you know that?" She grabbed it from my hands and set it on the table. She grabbed an expensive plate and it matched exactly with the cake.

———

"Now, it's time to cook." I cooked the noodles closely following Lilith's instructions while looking at my phone. Lilith was doing most of the cooking. After I finished with the noodles, I stir-fried the vegetables although I didn't know what I was doing. Lilith was thankful for my help, but told me to go sit and watch TV as the rest of the food was being prepared.

Before so, I set up the table while Lilith put together different salads, obsessed with making everything look perfect. At that moment, I remembered how Mom used to make us prepare for dinner which seemed to take longer than cooking.

I usually came late for dinner, which made Mom upset. I was such a child obsessed with playing football. However, it feels like I've matured with the whole adventure here, even if it was unfair.

"I think this will do." Staring at the decorated table, it was fully prepared. My mouth watered looking at it and I couldn't wait to dig in.

Lilith kept looking at the clock in the dining room. Her family were supposed to be here ten minutes ago. A slight concern that they might've bailed on her raised but I reminded her to have patience.

"They're outside. They're here!" She yelled out in excitement after being glued to the window for five minutes. I felt nervous myself and couldn't disappoint; she needed me now more than ever.

I joined her at the window. We saw them get out of the car. Her husband had dark black hair and looked well-kept. Lilith's teenage daughter wore her hair in a long ponytail while her son looked around thirteen years old and was holding a gaming device. They examined the house and then walked through the front gate. The expressions on their faces weren't reassuring, but they kept walking towards the porch.

Lilith rushed to the door, opening it. I stood there and watched. I admired her courage; it was beyond words.

"Juliette!" She embraced her daughter in a tight hug, letting the tears pour on their own. "Arthur, you got so big!" She hugged her son. It was an amazing scene seeing their family reunited. Her husband watched closely behind, but had no compassion on his face.

"Richard," She spoke between cries. The man simply greeted her and all of them came inside. The minute they looked around, they noticed me standing next to the dining table.

"Who's this?" Richard spoke in a loud manner.

"This is Abbasi. He is one of my good friends who works as a model and is here to help me explain some things." Her remarks made Richard look sickening.

"Are you serious? Even at this time, you bring one of your boy toys? I can't believe this." He threw his hands up in the air, frantic at what he saw. The kids didn't think much of it but watched their parents continue to fight which appeared to be the norm for them.

"It's not that, sir." I interjected. Richard looked at me as if he didn't want me to get involved, but that was the purpose of this dinner. "I'm here to explain what New Era did to me, Lilith and many others. Hopefully, you'll understand after hearing my story." I looked at him with compassion.

"I've prepared this food for you all, I'm glad you've joined us."

Lilith ushered the kids toward the table and they shook Abbasi's hand.

"We've missed you, Mom." Arthur commented, not

being able to part from his mother. I felt his pain. If only I had the chance to embrace my mother at the moment.

"I missed you too, sweetheart." She hugged him back and caressed Juliette's hand. It was that motherly love which cannot be missed for a long time.

Richard took a seat on the table without speaking. It felt like he didn't want to be here. He looked at me but I looked away, feeling under pressure. I kept silent until Lilith took her seat and started the conversation.

She couldn't part with her kids and caressed them until she made herself comfortable, not taking her eyes off them. "A lot of things happened since we last saw each other. What I did was a huge mistake, and now I'm only left with asking for your forgiveness." She lowered her eyes to her plate, still not being able to look at them in their faces.

My eyes bound to Richard who was crossing his arms but wasn't buying it. "You're crossing your lines now, Lilith," he spoke up as his eyes narrowed in on her. She couldn't help to put her hands over her face. It was a tense moment.

"New Era fooled her into a false contract. I know because I'm one of the models whom they exploited. They forced me into being a sex worker. Lilith was promised that her brand would be expanded if she was a sponsor of New Era. But she didn't know they had ulterior motives. Neither did I. Pauline, the owner blackmailed her as I was too." I couldn't believe I was speaking like this in front of her children, but Lilith didn't tell me to stop.

""I have sources that Pauline told the model Lilith was with that evening to cause an accident, so Lilith would pay her a large sum of money."

Richard was at a loss of words and the kids were as well.

"Benjamin told me he found the model you were with in the car with that night. He's alive and well, and we're hoping to get him to testify when we submit all our evidence to Interpol."

The only thing we heard next was a loud scream of joy.

Lilith could finally live a normal life again. Richard's eyes had began watering as he looked at his estranged partner now with loving eyes.

"Oh, Lilith." He embraced holding Lilith tightly. I saw in his eyes he'd never stopped loving her. It was truly a beautiful moment.

"Why did you keep this from me?" Her eyes were red from crying.

"I wanted to be 100 percent sure." She would've freaked out if she knew about this earlier. This was my gift for her cooperation.

"You're really cool, Abbasi." Arthur spoke up and gave me a thumbs up.

We all laughed. "You're welcome." I replied and then his sister Juliette turned towards me.

"Merci, Abbasi." She smiled. I nodded and smiled back. "It's my pleasure."

"Now, let's dig in." We did so, enjoying the food which was tasty. Later, Lilith served her husband and I wine, and we talked about everything from New Era, France to Cameroon. The kids were in the living room watching TV and once we were finished, we joined them. Somehow, as the evening went by, stories by Lilith became our entertainment.

"I remember this one time, Richard came to my door at 3 a.m. My whole family was sleeping, and he asked me out to go watch a movie with him."

"Back then, the cinemas showed the best movies and were open 24 hours. She closed the door in my face almost every time I asked her out." We all bursted into laughter. I wanted to hear more, but their kids were constantly complaining about changing the TV stations.

"By the way, Mom. Emma and I aren't speaking anymore. She got mad at me over a boy."

Lilith's face looked embarrassing. She appeared disappointed. "What happened? It's a shame! You were friends since kindergarten." She pouted and gave comfort to Juliette. "Friends come and go, I'm sure you will find better ones."

After a while of staying silent, I couldn't help but say something. "No need to worry. Your mother's right." Juliette nodded her head.

"What about you Abbasi? Tell us about your family." Richard rested his elbows on his knees, prepared to listen.

"Well, my father is a delivery man and Mom's a housewife."

"She must've spent her life raising a good young man like yourself." *I'm grateful for his kind remark.*

"Dad wasn't around, because he was always working. Over the years that has changed, he's played a larger role in us growing up." Keeping my eyes on the fireplace, I daydreamed the precious moments of my past.

"They must miss you very much."

"They do," I replied. "But Lilith here will help me put an end to this misery and help me get back home."

Richard, growingly proud of Lilith, was caressing her shoulder.

"We need confessions out of Marie and Leonarda."

Richard flinched at the mention of Leonarda's name. "I used to work with her, an absolute nightmare." He shook his head, trying to block out the memories of her. *Was she that bad? Sounds like she's big trouble.*

"Relax. We'll take her down. Justice will be served and they will go to prison where they belong" Lilith said.

We didn't stop chatting until it was almost 11 p.m. Ines would go ballistic for sure. I thought about bribing the security guard somehow in order not to tell her.

"I need to leave right away. I'll see you soon." I expressed while Richard shot up from his seat.

"We can give you a lift since we aren't sleeping here. I have work early in the morning."

"Thanks, Richard." We left out heading towards the car and Lilith gave me a big hug.

"Thank you for everything. You're the best."

"Don't mention it." It was what every human being would've done if in my position. I did what was right; I reunited a family.

The car ride to New Era was fast. I was with Arthur in the back seat and he kept blabbering about the recent game he had downloaded. I was so tired that I zoned out while some soft jazz was playing in the background.

Lilith told Richard to drop me off a few streets away at a gas station to pick up a bottle of beer for the security guard. Old guy works so hard, a cold one wouldn't hurt him. Working at that hellhole, it'll do him some good.

Once I was at the front gate; I saw the old guard sleeping behind the desk in his little glass box.

It was funny sight to see. I couldn't help but laugh and he woke up from my voice, jumping up. I walked over to him as he fixed his glasses, trying his best to look as if he was awake.

"It's me, Abbasi. The one you keep telling Ines about being late."

He squinted his eyes at me. "What do you expect? I'm just doing my job." His attitude changed the moment he saw a bottle of beer in my hands.

"This is for you. Maybe you'll keep this our little secret. Remember I caught you taking a nap on duty."

He thought about it but ultimately gave in. "We have a deal."

I handed him the beer and walked through the entrance, wishing him a good night.

The halls were empty and dark. I heard someone laughing, and it was coming from the lounge room. *Who was up at this time of night?* I couldn't help but to want to know who it was. I walked by, only to find Zane laughing alone. *Was he drunk?* I made a noise accidentally kicking the door, and it caught his attention. I cursed when he spotted me.

"There he is! The star himself came to visit me." His speech was slurred and once I came closer, a bottle of vodka in his hand looked almost empty. This is weird. He's getting drunk alone. I feel sorry for him, so let me help him get to our room.

"Come on buddy. Get up, you're drunk." I tried to grab a hold of his arm but he pulled away from me.

"Don't touch me, motherfucker." He shouted, pointing his finger at me.

I didn't listen and continued trying to grab him. He jerked back again, giving me a dirty look. I've never seen him look at me so savagely. "It's all your fault." He yelled. I looked around panicking if somebody heard us. I tried to calm him down but to no avail. "It was better when you weren't here. The attention was all on me. I was the best one model at New Era." His eyes were welling up with tears as he took another swing.

"Let's get out of here first, okay?" I calmly spoke.

Zane got up on his feet and fell down. He got back up and tried to swing at me but luckily; I dodged his fist punch. "Can you calm down?" I yelled at him. He wasn't listening.

"Why can't you go back to your hut in Afria?" He squinted his eyes, shaking his head.

"That's real racist, Zane. Don't make me fuck you up. I can tolerate your bullshit but not this." I couldn't care less if anyone hears me now. He made me vexed, and I couldn't hold back my anger any longer.

Zane stayed silent. His drunken posture was a terrible sight to see. I left him like that and went to the elevators. *"Fuck him."*

Most of the guys are fake tough guys here at New Era. I missed my friends back home. They're the realest. When I got back to the room, Jafari was in living room, watching TV.

"What's wrong now?" He said seeing my face drenched in anger.

"Nothing."

"If it's about Zane, you can chill. He's been screaming at everyone for the past two hours. Ines and Pauline left on a sudden business trip, so everyone's taking it easy."

"It's not my fault his mistresses want nothing to do with him. He called me a racist slur."

Jafari gaped, "That's cold, man. Fuck him." We chatted for a bit, and I didn't mention where I was earlier in the evening. I haven't told him about Lilith or Benjamin yet. They were my biggest secrets to bringing down this company.

Zane didn't come upstairs for the rest of the night

and I didn't care if he did or not. I fell asleep around 1 AM and hoped the next day would be better than this one.

9

MERDE

SHIT!

Two days after the Zane incident, I was awakened by Jafari's loud voice telling me to wake up. "What?" I snapped, angrily.

"Get up. Pauline is back and wants to see you. It must be big if the big boss's asking for you." He pulled the comforter off my bed.

"Yeah, right." I got dressed quickly, brushing my teeth. What does she want so early in the morning? I had plans for today, and if she assigned me work, I'd have to cancel my meeting with Lilith.

"Tell me the details later." I rolled my eyes at him and rushed out the door.

I greeted Trisha, and she almost dropped her drink, smiling and looking at me.

"I heard Pauline would like to see me, is she inside?"

"Yeah, go right in, Abbasi."

Swinging the door open, I walked into her office and

found there were around five models in front of her; including Zane and Daniel. Zane looked at me without emotion and I did the same. He probably felt sorry about his drunken rant on me two nights ago. *Who gives a damn?*

"Since all of you are here, I will start by congratulating you all and say you made it on the list of guests for Leonarda's big birthday party!" She clapped and the rest of the guys applauded. I nodded smiling. It wasn't something to celebrate. I watch the others as they were whistling; making a big deal out of it.

"First, you'll need to dress your best. Trisha will be giving you your suits in two days and you need to be extra early. Ines and I will be accompanying you. Just know the party will be hosted on a superyacht at the Cannes on the French Riviera. I hate to inform you but you are not allowed to drink anything other than champagne. You're representing New Era. We don't want you to make any bad impressions on these special guests. Do you understand?"

We nodded. "*A superyacht on the French Riviera?* Wow!" All of us exclaimed.

"Is everything crystal clear?" she asked once more, crossing her arms.

"Can we bring dates?" Daniel joked making us bust out in laughter.

Pauline didn't find it amusing, and she looked at him as if he was crazy. "No. It's only going to be five of you. That yacht will be filled with celebrities and influential people. Don't do anything stupid. I'm warning you." She walked over to him and put out her hand. Daniel lowered his head and kissed it. *"Oh my God!"*

"You're dismissed." She took a seat behind her desk. Lilith would be delighted as it meant we could proceed on with our plan.

Once we made it out into the hallway, the group was laughing at Daniel. I walked to the elevators and texted Lilith. We were scheduled to meet a few blocks away at our normal spot. She has been so overwhelmed by the reunion, she probably hasn't gotten full night of sleep yet.

I know she would be thrilled about me getting to Leonarda, but how would she get on the yacht with me? We had to figure something out because Leonarda's birthday party was in two days. She texted me saying she was at exact spot waiting for me. When I got there, she was talking to someone on the phone.

"I'll come take a look at it next week. I'm thinking about putting my house on the market. I doubt anyone will buy it. It's old and small. I'll still want to try though." I listened attentively. *Why was she planning on moving out after the reunion?* Lilith hung up after I almost fell asleep.

"How's life treating you?" I opened the conversation with.

She grinned. "Wonderful." Lilith seemed to be in good spirits.

"So, Marie is almost the last one. Do you know where we will find her?"

Lilith turned on the engine and backed out.

"We're going to her office."

I turned to her, shocked. *"What?"* I wasn't sure if I could proceed with this crazy ass idea.

"Unlike Amy, this woman has a lot of bodyguards, so it would be impossible to get her in this car."

"I don't know how I feel about this one."

"Come on. This is an easy one. You should be stressed about Leonarda. You'll have to work harder. Believe me!"

I almost forgot. "Speaking of Leonarda, guess who just got on the list of her birthday party?" I said pointing at myself, earning a big whoop from her.

"I knew you could do it!"

I shrugged like it wasn't a big deal.

"I'm one of Pauline's favourites." I felt proud of myself for once.

"No wonder."

"Why is that?"

"Nobody gets invited to a party like that easily. It's obvious you are one of her sweethearts."

"It's all about the money for her at the end of the day."

Lilith started driving as it would take time to get there since it was on the other side of Paris. We wore identical hats, hoping no one would recognize us. I listened to her instructions during the drive and planned on doing everything correctly. *We didn't need any fuckups.*

The building where Marie worked, Tour Total, was humongous. There were glass doors at the front entrance that opened instantly anytime it senses motion. We walked up to the receptionist desk after passing by some beautiful portraits, where again Lilith spoke.

"We're here to see Marie, the CEO of Le Marie Beauty. We don't have an appointment unfortunately, but please mention Pauline, the owner of the New Era modelling agency sent us." She didn't even give the receptionist a chance to talk. Lilith was professional. I remained silent next to her and before we knew it, the receptionist called Marie on her phone.

"You can proceed, this way." She got up from her seat and led us down a long corridor. "The last door on the left." She said giving us a warm smile and quickly returned up front.

"Abbasi, hurry up. We don't have all day." I didn't notice her already ahead of me. I hurried and we reached the front of Marie's office. I was nervous and she pulled me in front of her. I was the one to knock and would enter first.

"Come in!" She heard us at the door. I cursed silently and opened the door, revealing a beautiful woman in her forties standing, looking out of the windows of her office. "Bonjour Madame Marie, we're here on Pauline's behalf." I tried not to stutter. She then turned her attention to us, with a welcoming expression on her face.

"Take a seat." I was glad she didn't recognise Lilith

who was still wearing her hat. I didn't know when she would reveal herself but I played along.

"It's been a while since I saw her. How is she?" Marie said resting her elbows on the table, focusing her attention solely on me.

"She's fine. She sent us to find out how you would be dressing for Leonarda's birthday party." *I had messed up by saying that. It was the first thing that came to mind.*

"I'm not sure. But why didn't she ask me over the phone?" Her words slowed down as she began looking over at Lilith. I could feel her anger arising and I expected this to get sour any minute now.

"Okay, let's get this shit over with. We ask, you answer. Am I clear?" Lilith took off her hat and had pulled her gun out on Marie. The woman's eyes began rolling in confusion and she placed her hands up in the air.

"Don't hurt me. I'll do as you say, please." She was scared and Lilith ordered her to keep her hands on her desk, without moving. Lilith started recording and looked solely on Marie. The woman was terrified and I knew she would confess everything.

And she did. She admitted to paying for male escorts from New Era and forcing them to have sex against their wills. I was so sick of these people and the fact they could buy whomever and whatever they pleased. Suddenly, there was a loud knock on the door. "Lilith, hurry up." I whispered.

"Tell them you're busy, Marie, now or else you're dead!"

"Please come back. I'm in a meeting. Merci." Marie said in a pleading manner.

After thirty seconds or so, Lilith said, "Marie, we're done here. If you bring up this to anyone, I'll make sure this tape gets out to France 24." Lilith gave her a sarcastic smirk. I got up from my seat, ready to leave.

"Oh, and please tell your private security not to follow us. If I find that we are being trailed, I'll release this tape in a heartbeat."

"Ok" Marie said weeping.

We, then walked calmly to the front entrance and got back in our car safely.

Now we had recorded confessions on four of the women and getting Leonarda's would be the most difficult. "How will you get on that superyacht?" I wondered.

"Don't worry about me. I'll get in dressed as a waiter. You need to get her inside a room and turn your phone on to record the conversation. I won't be able to get too close to her." *That'll be suicide. How would I even find the opportunity to be in the same place as her? What happens if I fail?*

Blocking out those thoughts, I listened to her closely as she kept describing how we can proceed. I was getting edgy, and she saw it was time for me to go back. *How I would get Leonarda's confession at her birthday party? On a supery-*

acht filled with the most richest people in Paris? This is absolute madness.

The next thirty-six hours passed quickly. Trisha called me upstairs to get my suit while Jafari was staring at mine the entire evening. "Do you know what material this is? This is a three-thousand-euro suit, man!" I snatched it away from him as he kept putting his hands on it.

"It's not mine, boy. I'm borrowing it for tonight and don't want to mess it up."

"So, I guess the yacht will be packed with the most richest people in France. Do me a favour and add my name to your conversations?" he jokingly said.

"I'm trying to get evidence to shut this escort service down for good."

"Most of them will be drunk anyway, so relax, man."

He was right. But I wasn't there to mingle. I took a shower and got dressed, placing the suit on carefully. Ines would make me pay if I damaged it.

"How do I look?" I buttoned up the jacket and straightened the collar, checking myself out in the mirror.

"Boy, you look like a million dollars as they say in America."

"Merci, Beaucoup!"

The only thing missing was some good cologne. "Jafari, do you have some good smelling cologne, bro? Nothing strong."

"Here you go." Jafari sprayed me down with Yves Saint Laurent La Nuit De L'homme, almost drowning me in it. It was time to head out.

"Good luck." He crossed his fingers and walked me down to the main lobby and then went back upstairs. There was a black van waiting outside for us and I was the first one down. *If Pauline was here, she'd be upset.*

After fifteen minutes, the four others finally came downstairs including Zane, who got dressed in Daniel's room for some reason. We wore matching suits, but each had different stitches. Zane looked at me and didn't say a word. I didn't either.

We drove off. I didn't talk as I listened to the guys and their silly jokes.

"We're getting drunk for sure tonight fellas" Zane whispered.

"Yeah, right" I said to myself.

Once we arrived to the port of the French Riviera, I saw the superyacht's lights beaming in all directions. It was gigantic and it could probably host around two or three hundred inside easily. Some guests had already began showing up, but we waited outside for Pauline and Ines to arrive.

The two snakes showed up fifteen minutes later in a white limousine. *Man, they just got to show off.* Damn, it wasn't their birthday parties for God's sake.

"Boys, you look perfect. I'm proud of you. Now, let's go aboard." Ines was wearing a printed silk dress by the Kooples while Pauline wore a mink coat from A.P.C and a flashy dress. *They looked like they were going out clubbing to be honest.*

The yacht was spectacular with security with white

earphones guarding every inch of it. I had seen nothing like it before. The hour, we travelled to the Cannes felt worth it. When we got to the boat's bridge to come onboard, there were men dressed in tuxedos who asked for our names.

"Abbasi Ademola." I replied, looking around mesmerised by the boat's scenery. These guests here are worth lots of money. *Maybe they had enough money to sponsor every country in Africa.* Suddenly, I felt afraid, not knowing if I could go through with all this. *Where's Lilith? How much longer will this take?* The many questions that popped up in my head at the wrong moment of time.

"This way, Messieurs." We were seated at a table near the rear of the yacht. It wasn't the best place to be, but not unusual. Pauline and Ines were glamorously walking side by side, with some other female and male guests accompanying them. Pauline definitely wouldn't sit with us. It would make her look inferior. The waiters came over to our table a few minutes later and served us champagne. All the boys clinked glasses with one another. I had no choice but to do the same.

"Abbasi, is there something wrong? Daniel spoke to me for the first time in ages.

"I chilling, that's all." Daniel nodded while sipping on his drink.

Soft jazz was playing in the background and everyone all the sudden got up to dance in pairs. We stayed back and watched. In between the guests, was Leonarda dancing with her husband. She was wearing a silk sparkling ballgown. They were right when they said she was the oldest of the millionaire convicts. Her face looked mushed, probably injected with Botox because it wasn't even moving with her body.

The waiter came over again bringing us glasses of scotch this time. "Remember what Pauline said?" I warned the guys and of course, Zane had to show off.

"It's none of your business what we drink Abbasi. Finish your water."

"Haha" the guys cheered.

I wasn't in the mood to argue, so I kept my eye out on Leonarda. Soon enough, the crowd began singing 'Happy Birthday' to her as the temperature inside got cooler. Pauline ordered the yacht's staff to close the doors.

———

I have to do this soon or else. Ines was like a hawk spying on us at our table. *How were we going to pull this off?* I didn't see Lilith anywhere and was worried she didn't make onboard. *What if she got discovered?*

"Excuse me." I yelled after no one seemed to move to let me out. Once I got inside the bathroom, I called Lilith.

She picked up. "Why aren't you doing anything? I'm in the kitchen doing tons of work. I didn't sign up for this shit." She sounded angry.

"I am, but I don't know how. The woman won't let go her husband!" I complained.

"Okay, listen. She probably will go to her quarters to relax sometime soon. She's too old to be out here dancing plus I heard she takes medication."

"Just find out where her quarters are and post up somewhere close by. You'll see as the night drags on. She can't hang with these young people. Believe me!" She suddenly whispered, indicating someone was coming her way.

"Got it." I hung up. I only needed to have patience. Pauline and Ines were continually looking in our direction while I waited for Leonarda. I walked away to the other side of the yacht; resting on the door and staring into the moonlight, many couples passed by and right when I was getting comfortable, Leonarda herself came alone into my area. She looked drained, barely able to walk. Her husband wasn't around, so it seemed to be the perfect opportunity. I texted Lilith: *"I'm with Leonarda."* Then, I quickly opened the app on my phone to record and placed it inside my suit jacket.

"Do you need help, Madame Leonarda?" I was now next to her, clutching her arm.

"It's all right but since you offered, can you walk with me and hand me my medication inside my personal quarters?"

"Bien sûr." I smiled leading her. When we arrived to Room 4, I shut the door and helped Leonarda towards the bed. "They're inside my handbag." She said breathing heavily. "Right over there on top of the drawer."

I handed her the bag and then went to the kitchen to get her a glass of water. I texted Lilith: *"Room 4."* And then came back and watched Leonarda chug down the water.

"Merci."

I knew time was ticking and Lilith hasn't texted me back. I must keep our conversation going a little bit longer. "This superyacht is very beautiful, Madame Leonarda. You have good taste. It must have cost a fortune." I said, hoping she would take her time on answering me.

"It did. My husband bought it for me years ago. I haven't seen you around before. By the way, who are you?"

"I'm Abbasi Ademoli, one of the new models from New Era, Pauline's agency."

"Have you been in one of my private sessions before?" She took out a cigarette, offering me one. I kindly declined and then answered, "No, I haven't, Madame."

"Good. I could use some fresh juice. Get undressed, my boy. I have something I would like to give you as a present."

"Madame, you are not feeling well. Don't let me burden you." I responded.

"My boy, you have earned this opportunity. Now, do as I say."

Suddenly, there was a loud knock on the door and she ordered me to see who it was. I walked towards it and behold; it was no one other than Lilith.

"Is the witch asleep yet?" I put my finger to my mouth to hush. *Oh shit! No, she didn't say that.*

Next thing, I heard was Leonarda's voice. "Stop right there where you are and don't move." She pointed a big gun at us. I took a step back, terrified. *Our plan had now gone down the drain.*

"Close the door now."

I did, not knowing what to expect next.

"Lilith, you're a fool to have come here and convinced this boy to help you in your pettiness. I had a feeling that something fishy was going on the moment, this boy refused my call. I will kill you both and have your bodies dumped into the ocean. And guess what? No one will know. No one." She said those words, loud and clear. *We would surely die here.*

"It's over for you, Leonarda, you can say goodbye to this world you created of extortion and greed. Those brick walls will be crumbling on you for the rest of your old life." Just as Lilith said that, she pulled out her gun, pushing me out of the way.

Then at that very moment, they fired at the same time.

At first, I felt no pain, only the distant cry coming from Lilith. I realised it was the end as I began seeing lights. The burning sensation suddenly jolted through my body and all I could hear were the loud cries outside of the door. *I was dying.*

10

___

FIN

THE END

A sharp pain in my left arm was the only thing I could feel at the moment. *"Abbasi."* I heard Lilith's voice close by. I didn't have the strength to get up just yet. I was comfortable; falling back to sleep, until she calmly called my name again.

"Abbasi," she whispered. This time, I slowly opened my eyes; squinting until the view of the speaker's face became clear. I saw a woman's face. *It's Lilith.* She had a wide smile on her face. *So, I didn't die.* I tried sitting up, but the pain in my arm, stopped me from doing so.

"Where am I?" I asked hoarsely. It felt as if I was waking up from a coma.

"You're at Saint-Louis Hospital. You've been in and out of it for the last two days. But look who came to see you." I could now see clearly. My eyes shifted to a large figure behind her. It was Jafari smiling at me.

"Hey, man. How are you feeling, big guy? You're the man, bro."

I smiled back.

"What happened after I got hit? How am I still alive? How did I get to the hospital?"

"The bullet just grazed you, Abbasi. It will heal in no time. You're lucky to be alive. God's watching over you." As Lilith spoke, I looked at my arm and saw it wrapped in a bandage.

"Merci Beaucoup." And I meant it, sincerely.

With Jafari's help, I was able to sit up. Then, I saw Zane standing behind Jafari. What I really wanted were my parents to be here, not this guy.

"Zane, what are you doing here?"

He lowered his head, and then looked at me. "I guess I was wrong after all. I'm sorry brother for being so much of a dick." His admission made me laugh so hard. *What happened to Leonarda? New Era?* I don't see anyone else around. I still was at lost about what happened.

"What in the world happened?" I asked. The room became silent as Lilith pulled out her phone and opened a website she had bookmarked:

"Pauline Berger, CEO of New Era Modelling Agency was arrested two nights ago on the yacht of CEO business woman Leonarda Denis, along with the rest of her senior staff. They're being charged with human trafficking, racketeering, money laundering and pandering. It was discovered that Pauline Berger and her assistants, named in this indictment, Ines and Francois,

exploited models to a group of the agency's made-up sponsors. Leonarda Denis has been additionally charged with two counts of attempted murder on top of other charges. As well, Amy Fabien, Marie Herbert, Amanda Legrand and Katherine Monet are being charged with solicitation, pandering and more charges are expected to be announced. There will be a full investigation into this matter and expect full transparency in its process."

Lilith, then showed the video of Pauline, Ines, Francois and Trisha being arrested, along with Leonarda. Amy Fabien is on the run, but eventually will be caught. Katherine, Marie and Amanda turned themselves in, and New Era's doors were now closed down forever.

"Since you don't have any documents to return home, I contacted the human rights organization, Climade, to help get you a new passport, exit visa and legal representation for a civil suit."

"Are you sure it's safe to leave?" I wanted to make sure that I was safe because these criminals had connections.

She nodded. "I wouldn't send you anywhere without researching first. They're legit, no need to worry." At that moment, I felt relieved. I would be going home.

"They'll come and pick you up from my house after you're discharged. Jafari brought some food for us to eat."

"Are you staying?" I directed my question towards Zane and Jafari.

"Yes, we're staying. We're going to rent an apartment

and be full-time models at Sarah's agency." I was glad they'll be together. I couldn't stop thinking about my family back home. I couldn't stay even if I wanted to.

For the rest of the day, we ate and had long talks about the whole ordeal. I didn't want to leave these guys, but I had to. I'd never forget this episode and felt like I got something positive out of it.

A few members of Climade came to Lilith's house in the evening and patiently waited for me outside.

"Call me when you get home. Don't you dare forget about me."

Lilith, Richard and the kids were sobbing and I couldn't hold back my tears. I finally gave in. "Never." I said. I hugged Zane, Jafari, Lilith and everyone but was speechless. I'd see them again. I was sure about that.

I got in the van, and it was ready to drive off almost immediately. In the backseat, along with two others, I sat quietly staring out the window. My friends for life waved as we pulled off. I'd remember them for as long as I live.

———

Two days had passed since I got on the plane from Paris to Cameroon. Luckily, they expedited my passport from the embassy, so I could board the first plane leaving. I was so exhausted and only wanted to sleep in my bed at home. The plane was landing, and for the first time in three and a half months, I got a glimpse of Mother Cameroon.

I missed her, and was beaming from ear to ear, eager to get out of Paris. I telephoned my parents at Climade and told them I was coming home for good. They said that they will be at the airport when I arrived.

Once we landed, I grabbed my bags from the overhead bin and was left the plane, passing endless halls and finally at the escalator. There was a crowd waiting for their loved ones, and then I saw my family members, waving at me. Imani had a banner in her hand saying 'Welcome Home, Abbasi. You're a hero.' I smiled and ran towards them. Dad embraced me in a long hug which Mom and Imani joined in.

"I'm so glad you made it back safely." Dad tightened his grip around me.

I could barely breathe. "I made it back safely, Dad. It was a hell of a journey." I then glanced at Imani, "Isn't this a bit too much?" I remarked, she laughed.

"Oh, shut up." She hugged me again and then my eyes set on Mom.

She was in tears at the sight of her son. I comforted her by hugging her.

"Did you miss me?" I whispered. She nodded repeatedly, not being able to let go. *I was finally home. I was finally at peace.*

"They didn't do anything to my baby, did they?" She said touching my face, and I shook my head in denial.

"No, Mama" The details of the ordeal she didn't need to know.

None of us couldn't calm her excitement making it

back home in Dad's truck. Once we arrived, our neighbours were waiting outside of their compounds to greet me. It was a joyous occasion I never expected.

Mom hurried straight to the kitchen and began prepping. She already started cooking my favourites. *I missed her food.* Nobody can cook better than her. Dad told me he got a promotion at his job last week and his health was getting better. All good news to hear. My sister Imani came back to visit from university just to see me. At this moment, I realised how much family is important.

I helped Mom set the plates on the table, and then she told me to go rest. Should I go and visit my friends while the food is being prepared? It had been a while since I had seen them. I didn't send them a single message while I was in Paris.

Everyone on the streets greeted me as I walked through the neighbourhood even the small boys playing football in the roadways. *Did they hear about what happened? Maybe? Maybe not?* If they did, I'm glad no one said anything. *Just keep pretending like you don't know. I'm fine with that.* I reached our neighbourhood's football field and watched some of my boys playing from a distance.

Demond, Sudi and Tayo were running up and down, but stopped once they saw me.

"Abbasi?" Sudi yelled.

I screamed in joy and ran towards them. *"That's right, the man himself."*

Demond cursed, not expecting me home so soon. We embraced in a group hug.

"I'm surprised you made it back alive. I heard you were fucking millionaires over there. It must have been fun." Demond commented.

"How the hell did you know about that?" I replied rolling my eyes.

"We saw something on Facebook that mentioned your name as a sex trafficking survivor. Good thing, they didn't post your face."

I rolled my eyes as we laughed. "Good Lord. I'm so grateful for that. But, about that football you're holding, I hope I didn't damage your reputation by leaving you in charge of the team while I was gone." I snatched the ball from Tayo's hands and started dribbling.

I missed playing. Should I play right away? Coach would be mad if he knew I was back home so early. In Africa, if you come back from Europe or America early, you're frowned upon.

"Not at all. People still curse at us because we've been losing but now we have you back. Things will get better."

I missed those times and now realised how important friends were. We laughed and then I had something to say. "Enough of the rubbish, let's play so I can show you how it's done." I kicked the ball onto the field and they followed me.

As the days went on, I slowly starting building my

self-esteem back. It wasn't meant for me to be a model. Playing football was my joy. As much as I would love to go to other places in the world, without football, I would feel lost.

I learned how to cherish every moment in life and value new friendships. I got a glimpse of how life was outside of Africa and was grateful for the opportunity.

I'm not a loser but a fighter who escaped trafficking; many have not and will not. I am thankful to God as he had given me the strength to do anything.

As humans, we all made mistakes, and I made a bad one by rushing success. The point of life is to learn from your mistakes. I know my name would carry off in Cameroon's streets for as long as I live. When my story finally comes out, it'll be a big deal here and I'm glad I made it home in one piece. *Guess what?* I still have money left in my account and a civil case pending against New Era, so I wasn't dumb after all.